THE POTKIN AND STUBBS TRILOGY
BY SOPHIE GREEN

Potkin and Stubbs
The Haunting of Peligan City
Ghostcatcher

SOPHIE GREEN

Illustrated by
K. J. Mountford

Piccadilly
PRESS

First published in Great Britain in 2020 by
PICCADILLY PRESS
80-81 Wimpole St, London W1G 9RE
www.piccadillypress.co.uk

A CIP catalogue record for this book
is available from the British Library.

ISBN: 978-1-848-12859-0
Also available as an ebook

1

Typeset by Palimpsest Book Production Limited,
Falkirk, Stirlingshire

Printed and bound in Great Britain by Clays Ltd, Elcograf S.p.A.

MIX
Paper from
responsible sources
FSC® C018072

Piccadilly Press is an imprint of Bonnier Books UK
www.bonnierbooks.co.uk

For Luke

Chapter 1

Chinatown

Private Investigator Abe Mandrel gazed past the plastic coconuts dangling from his rear-view mirror, through the rain-splattered windscreen, and then down into his coffee. He tightened the grip of the new cup-holder attachment on his Swiss Army hand and took a tentative sip.

Chinatown's lights dazzled behind him. The rain roughed up the puddles and scattered the reflected neon of the signs for every kind of noodle bar. Red silk lanterns, faded pink, were strung across the road like bunting, and the aroma of sesame and soy carried all the way to where Abe's Ford Zodiac was parked shoulder to shoulder with the kerb, in the shadow between street lamps.

With his trilby tilted down low, all that could be seen of Abe was a hat, a heavy, stubbled jaw and a grim, set mouth. On the passenger seat, his small, sand-coloured mongrel, sniffed the air and let out a faint whine.

Abe tilted his wristwatch towards the lights and said, 'We'll give him another few minutes, Margaret.'

The house across the street was in darkness. Number forty-one was tall, thin and leaning slightly to one side. It was weather-boarded, like it was made of matchsticks, with steps up to the front and alleys on both sides.

Abe watched the ragged net curtains swell mysteriously in the windows. 'Come on, kid,' he muttered under his breath. A gold-coloured lucky cat sat on the windowsill with its paw

raised, though whether in greeting or warning Abe couldn't tell.

He angled the rear-view mirror to focus on the nearest chop suey restaurant. His stomach growled and Margaret frowned at it.

'If he's not out in five, I'm sending you in.'

Margaret looked purposefully ahead. She licked her nose to keep it sharp. The curtains in the window fluttered; the lucky cat's paw swung. Abe peered closer. 'What's he doing?' His eyes were drawn to the cat waving hypnotically to him. Margaret's ears had pricked up.

'What is it, girl?' Abe turned to face forward again, scanned the road ahead and then checked the rear-view mirror. A parking space that had been empty was now filled by a car, one that had rolled in with no lights.

He saw a glimmer of moonshine on a sleek-looking bonnet, then there was a sharp rap on the window. He whipped around to see a face jump into view inches away from his own.

'Gah!' Abe yelled, flipping the contents of

his mug into the air and catching it on his shirt.

Lil Potkin gestured impatiently for him to open the window. Abe glared at her as he wound the handle. She was wearing a navy fishing hat pulled down low to hide her bobbed hair and cup-handle ears, but the signature yellow rain mac gave her away every time.

As soon as the window had dropped irreversibly into its slot in the door, Lil popped her head through it and scanned the car. 'Nedly isn't with you?'

Abe stopped grinding his teeth just long enough to say, 'He's working. Are you here to – ?'

Lil cut him off. 'We have to get him out. It's Ghostcatcher. They're right behind us.'

'What!' Abe sat forward quickly, sloshing the coffee dregs over his sleeve. 'How did they – ?'

'There's no time! He can't be here when they arrive!' Lil insisted. 'Which house?'

Abe pointed across the road with his cup. 'The one with the lucky cat. But it's empty; he's –'

Lil interrupted again. 'If it's empty, then who called the Haunting Hotline?' She gave Abe an exasperated look. 'I've got to warn him! You cover for me.'

'Wait! Where's Quake?'

'She's still in the car. I'm just checking the back way for signs of the haunting. Come on, let's go!'

Abe only had a second to look confused before Margaret trod in his wet lap as she clambered over him and then jumped out of the window, following Lil across the street.

Lil crouched and ran quickly down the alleyway between the buildings. Margaret scampered ahead with her nose to the ground and then disappeared into the crawl space under the house.

The back garden was moonlit and festooned with abandoned shuttlecocks and tennis balls. A rusted swing was overturned and the decomposing wicker garden furniture looked like it was sinking into the ground.

Lil waded knee-deep through the long wet grass and then ran up the steps to the porch. The old wood was slippery with algae. 'Nedly?' she whispered as loudly as she dared.

The nearest window was painted shut. She tried the back door, rattling the knob back and forth and then, glancing furtively left and right, she applied a bit of shoulder pressure, but it was definitely locked. Lil was beginning to panic now; she cupped her hands round her eyes and peered into the darkness.

The room was fuzzily dark and made ghostly by the net curtains, which cast shadows like torn spiderwebs. Pale sheets covered the furniture and dust bunnies rolled across floorboards. Lil knelt down at the keyhole and hissed, 'Nedly!'

Margaret's sharp warning bark cut through the night followed by the crackling sound of tyres on a wet road, and then silence.

There was no more time for subtlety. Lil

thumped loudly on the glass. 'Nedly! It's time to go!'

The hair on her neck prickled and rose in the wave of dread that Lil had got used to ignoring now. There was a sound like a pebble being dropped into a glass of water and Nedly appeared at the door.

His large eyes looked like hollows in his pale, thin face and a lock of his roughly cut hair fell over his forehead.

Lil half shouted: 'Quick! You have to leg it.'

On the street there was the sound of car doors slamming.

'Ghostcatcher are here! Already?' Nedly gasped.

'You can make it. Just go!'

Nedly ran into the middle of the garden. He started one way and then panicked and turned another. He looked back at Lil; she jabbed her thumb in the direction of the street and he gulped, nodded and then ran through the fence at the side of the yard.

Lil puffed out her cheeks, took another deep

breath to slow down her heart and make herself seem calm and then, keeping close to the shadows of the house next door, she snuck back down the alleyway to watch.

The silver Ghostcatcher van had parked diagonally to block any traffic, its hazard lights pulsing the street with orange. Three figures in white hazmat suits, protective boots and helmets with reflective visors were strapping harnesses onto each other's backs, battery packs sprouting wires channelled into the shoebox-sized consoles that they carried.

With synchronised strides they took the stairs up to the front door. One knelt down, pulled something out of their pocket, squashed it into the lock and then they all turned away. A puff of smoke later and the door swung open and dropped off its hinges and the figures stepped inside.

Lil skirted behind the van to catch up with Marsha Quake, who had left her car, a smart Mercury coupe, and under the cover of a neat black umbrella was stalking towards Abe's battered Zodiac. Quake's long red hair was twisted up into a chignon and hidden under the hood of the silk scarf that was wound round her neck, but despite the elegance of her outfit her green velvet trouser suit was wearing thin at the elbows and her brogues were looking tired. She wore dark glasses and the colour of her lipstick was so deep it was almost brown.

The name Marsha Quake was an alias; all the *Klaxon* reporters had them. Lil's mother was known as Randall Collar; Lil herself was Stellar Darke. Their real names were kept secret to protect their identities for fear that City Hall would find a way to silence them, as it had with the intrepid reporter Roland Selznick.

Previously Lil had only known of Quake as the author of her favourite book, *McNair and the Free Press*, a biography of her childhood hero. Since then Lil had discovered that McNair was a fiction, a fake name that, for a while, had protected not one but a whole group of reporters when speaking the truth became too dangerous and the freedom of the press was outlawed.

'Absolom Mandrel.' Quake addressed Abe in her usual clipped, confident tone and then propped herself up against the car beside him. 'We must stop meeting like this.'

Abe was leaning stiffly against the bonnet, his arms folded over his coffee-stained shirt. He clenched and unclenched his jaw a few times and then tried to smile with it. 'Marsha Quake. What a coincidence.'

As she approached them Lil made her own half-hearted attempt at a look of surprise. It was becoming an old routine.

When Logan Mackay, librarian and the editor of the *Klaxon*, finally agreed to take on Lil as a trainee reporter, everyone expected that she would want to work with her mother, Naomi, investigating the political corruption stories that Randall Collar was famous for, but Lil had surprised them all by asking to shadow Quake instead.

Lil's choice had been clear. Ghostcatcher was

Quake's story. Lil had to follow it to ensure she always got an early alert about Ghostcatcher's movements through the radio scanner on Quake's car. This way she was able to dog their every call-out without arousing suspicion and arrive in time to warn Nedly to flee whenever they got too close. The irony was that Naomi had only passed up on the first Ghostcatcher scoop to spend more time with Lil, but things didn't turn out the way that either of them had hoped and her plan had backfired.

Quake arched an eyebrow at Abe and said breezily, 'The *Klaxon* is here because Ghostcatcher was alerted to some haunting activity at this address and we're investigating. How about you?' She opened a bag of nuts and passed them around.

Abe took one, ignored the question and asked one of his own. 'Who do you think called it in?' He squinted up and then down the darkened street. 'The place looks empty to me.'

Quake chewed distractedly. 'You tell me; you were here first. Care to comment, detective?'

'I was just passing.'

'You were parked when we pulled up.'

'It was a slow pass. I was considering getting some noodles.'

Lil huddled under Quake's umbrella; rain trickled off Abe's trilby and fell to the ground in front of him in threads. They all stood facing number forty-one and watched with interest. The windows lit up, glowing green with a ghostly light, like a haunted house at the funfair.

Quake turned to Lil. 'Find anything interesting out the back?'

Lil shrugged. 'I don't think anyone lives there. The door was locked but it all looked calm inside,' she added. 'My money is on another false alarm.'

Quake sucked some air through her teeth. 'There's got to be some reason they came out here. What do you say, Mandrel? Since I've been on this story everywhere I look you're there. What's your angle? Did you get a tip-off?'

Abe rubbed his cheek with his rubber palm.

'We got a lead on another matter but turns out it was a squib.'

'Here they come!' Lil straightened up, ready for business, as the scientists filed out of the building through the now permanently open doorway, their shoulders sagging, the consoles hanging down from their straps.

'Have you got a handle on this lot yet?' Abe murmured to Quake, keeping the brim of his hat low as he watched them make their way towards the van. 'What was their background before City Hall put them on the payroll? Eggheads?'

'Something like that.' Quake's sunglasses hid her eyes and a good deal of her face. She gave a nod and Lil pulled out her notepad, flicked it to the right page and gave Abe the lowdown.

'That first one is Magdalena Virgil.' As Lil spoke, Virgil climbed down the steps, undid a strap to release her helmet, removed it and shook out her long steel-grey hair. Her thick black brows were arched over piercing eyes. 'She's a maverick physicist.'

Virgil was followed by a tall man who removed his own helmet to reveal a closely shaved head, circular copper-wire-framed glasses and a generous mouth and nose. Round his neck was a second strap, which held a two-handled device, like a large macro-lens camera, which he was using to scan back and forth across the street. 'Arcos Marek,' Lil whispered. 'Quantum engineer.'

The last of the trio was already carrying his helmet under one arm. He had an asymmetrical bob of soft bouncing curls and a wide forehead which tapered all the way down to a little square dimpled chin. 'Laszlo Yossarian,' Lil reported. 'Experimental philosopher.'

As Yossarian approached the van he turned his head slightly and their eyes met. Lil thought she saw a smile.

She looked at Abe and Quake but neither had clocked it.

Virgil opened the sliding van door and took the weight of Yossarian's backpack as he shook his shoulders free of the harness, but Marek bypassed them completely and kept walking; his eyes were glued to the device in his hands.

Virgil called out as he passed them, 'It's off, Marek. You're going to have to recalibrate.'

But Marek ignored her and continued walking slowly towards Lil, muttering, 'Something caused the spike.' And then more loudly, 'It's here, Virgil!' Holding the apparatus in front of him like a divining rod, he started tweaking the dials. 'I'm picking up a residual EMF trace.'

'It's not working properly,' Virgil snapped. 'Leave it.'

Marek turned and looked up the street. Quake regarded him, one eyebrow curved with interest as he wandered past. Lil watched with mounting panic. He was heading towards Quake's Mercury.

'Hey, professor!' Lil blurted desperately. 'We have some questions for you.'

Ghostcatcher were notoriously wary of the press. Although Lil and Quake had been observing them for weeks they had never attempted an interview. These scientists didn't like questions if someone else was asking them.

Quake turned her eyebrow on Lil and one side of her mouth went up in an amused smile.

But Marek ignored her and called over his shoulder. 'It's a clear signal, Virgil. I'm sure of it.'

'Time to go, Marek. That means now!' Virgil insisted.

Reluctantly Marek turned and made his way past Lil and back to where Virgil was stripping the harness from her own shoulders before hurling it into the back of the van and slamming the door loudly.

'Hey,' Quake called out to Lil. 'If we're going to do this, let's go straight to the boss.' She darted towards Virgil. Casting a last relieved look back at the Mercury, Lil quickly selected a pencil, spun it once between her fingers and then joined Quake at the van.

Virgil dodged past them but Quake pursued her to the driver's side with Lil hot on her heels. 'Did you find anything in the house, Professor Virgil?'

Virgil paused with her hand on the doors. She glanced sharply at them, pursing her lips. 'We found a small scruffy dog.'

Lil cut in: 'A stray maybe? Do you think that's what caused the panic? Someone heard it howl, thought it was a spook and called you?'

Virgil's gaze lasered past Lil and locked on to the Zodiac where Margaret was sitting bolt upright in the front seat staring purposefully out of the windscreen. Her eyes narrowed as she saw Abe leaning against the bonnet. She called out to him, 'Haven't I seen you somewhere before?'

Abe dropped his chin, shading his eyes under the brim of his hat. 'I've got one of those faces.' He exchanged a quick glance with Lil and then got into his car. After a couple of strained engine sounds the Zodiac bunny-hopped away, sputtering black exhaust fumes behind it.

Virgil unlocked the van door and yanked it open.

'Has Ghostcatcher had any success in

apprehending a ghost since the doll hospital case?' Quake asked quickly.

The professor climbed in behind the steering wheel. 'There is only one ghost that we're looking for.'

'And when does your contract with City Hall expire?'

'No comment.'

Lil tried again. 'What do you think of the *Herald* coverage on the so-called Final Ghost, Professor? The spook they claim has been stalking Peligan City.'

Virgil frowned. 'I don't read it.'

Lil nodded approvingly and then gave her the Penetrating Squint. 'What would you say are your chances of catching him?'

Virgil returned Lil's Squint with an ice-cold stare. 'I'd say ninety-nine per cent.'

Quake dropped her chin and peered over her sunglasses. 'Can I quote you on that?'

Virgil turned the key firmly but paused just before she shut the door on them to reply: 'Absolutely.'

Chapter 2

The Final Ghost

The silver Mercury Coupe sped away through the city with Marsha Quake behind the wheel and Lil belted in beside her, riding low in the bucket seats. A police scanner was fitted into the dashboard where the radio would normally be and every few seconds Lil twisted the dial to check for signals in the static. The scanner had been on the blink ever since they pulled out of Chinatown due to the proximity of Nedly who, unbeknownst to Quake, had tucked himself into the narrow space behind Lil's seat and the parcel shelf.

'Ninety-nine per cent chance!' said Quake with a smirk. She had exchanged her dark glasses for clear ones and her long eyelashes shielded her green eyes as she stared through the unrelenting rain that was pelting the windscreen. 'We'll see. They've not even come close in weeks, as far as I can tell.'

'I don't believe them,' said Lil stubbornly.

'They sounded pretty confident, though,' Quake mused. She clung expertly to the bends as they snaked south towards the river, her hands clad in tan-leather driving gloves, the wind streaming through the rear window vents rippling her headscarf.

'A ninety-nine per cent chance of what?' Nedly whispered right in Lil's ear, making her jump, which caused Quake to swerve the car, hitting the kerb before bouncing back into the road.

Lil shivered uncontrollably. 'Sorry!' she said to Quake, giving Nedly a stern look out of the corner of her eye. 'I'm just a bit chilly.'

'S'OK,' said Quake, flicking a concerned glance at her and ramping up the car heater a couple of notches. 'I'm freezing too tonight.'

'Sorry,' Nedly winced, flattening himself back against the parcel shelf.

'Anyway, you have to hand it to them.' Quake continued where she had left off. 'Ghostcatcher, I mean. They've had nothing but misses lately and yet they still make it sound so . . .'

'Inevitable,' Lil murmured, and she stared out of the window at the glow of the city centre as it came into view, like a single ember burning in a pit of black ash. 'I bet it's just talk.'

'What's inevitable?' Nedly persisted, leaning carefully forward again.

Lil flashed her eyes at him. *Tell you later.*

'Well, I *hope* they have something,' said Quake. 'Otherwise this story is going to run out of legs. This is the third false alarm this week. Aside from the fall in the serious crime rate immediately after they busted those ghosts at the doll hospital, the whole thing is starting to look thin on facts. Ghostcatcher's own so-called readings are the only evidence that there even is another ghost, but if that's true then what's the problem? They caught the others easily enough.'

Lil snorted at this and rolled her eyes comically at Nedly who grinned and leant further forward again. Ghostcatcher had only ever caught one ghost: Mr Grip. Lil, Abe, Margaret, Nedly and Naomi had got rid of all the others, but their part in the drama had remained a secret.

Quake sighed thoughtfully. 'Everything is pointing towards it being a hoax, except my instinct tells me that Peligan City is still haunted. Every now and again things just feel really creepy, and I can't explain it.' She shivered violently.

Nedly retreated as quickly as he could, tucking himself into the furthest corner. His arms were wrapped round his legs and his cheeks were dark with embarrassment. Lil tried to catch his eye but he was staring fixedly out of the window.

She flumped back in her seat. 'If it's just the creeps, then it's no big deal, is it? I mean, you couldn't say that he's doing any harm.'

Quake was quiet as she took the East Bridge over the Kowpye River and Lil looked out at the water rippling grey in the moonlight. Finally, as they pulled into the slower traffic heading downtown, Quake spoke again: 'So, what makes you think it's a he?'

'What?' Lil's ears flamed red.

'Just now, and talking to Virgil earlier, you asked what were their chances of catching "him".'

'I didn't mean anything by it. Could be a she,' said Lil. 'Just not an "it".'

Quake considered this. 'That might be an interesting story in itself. If we could find out who the Final Ghost was before they died, then maybe they could work out how to catch it.'

Lil looked back over her shoulder. Nedly was still staring out of the small corner window as they passed beneath the streetlights. She turned back to Quake. 'You said yourself, the serious crime rate has fallen. Nothing dangerously spooky has happened so . . .' She let the statement hang. 'Why don't they give it a rest? Then maybe we could work on something else.'

Quake dropped through the gears and pulled on to Spooner Row. She brought the Mercury to an abrupt standstill outside the Nite Jar Cafe. 'Bored already?' She gave Lil a jokey smile. 'Look, if this ghost is out there, it's a story; if it's not out there and City Hall are knowingly using it as a distraction, it's a story. Either way, we have to follow where it leads – we're reporters: that's what we do.'

Lil paused in the doorway of the Nite Jar to pull off her dripping raincoat.

'Sorry I made you jump in the car,' Nedly said. Lil batted the apology away with a sprinkling of rainwater. 'But what was there a ninety-nine per cent chance of again?' He blinked at her earnestly.

Lil gripped her coat by the collar and then turned her back on him, and slowly hung it over one of the hooks on the rack by the counter. She paused before she let go of it, and said, 'Ninety-nine per cent chance that the ghost is real. That's all.' Then she turned to face him and smiled and he grinned back, looking relieved. 'Come on, they're waiting for us.'

Abe and Margaret were already sitting in the booth. Abe had ordered a strong black coffee, a bowl of water for Margaret, a mug of hot chocolate for Lil and a plate of custard tarts. There was a copy of the *Herald* on the table. Abe covered it with his trilby when he saw Lil approach.

While she waited for Nedly to take a seat, Lil peeled off her hat and rubbed her ears to get some life back into them and then slipped in beside him.

Abe had buttoned his jacket as high as it would go and turned the lapels up to try to hide the caramel-coloured coffee stain that had soaked through his shirt. Lil grimaced apologetically at him, took a custard tart and then glanced over her shoulder to check they were alone. When she was sure no one was in earshot she said: 'That was too close.'

Abe nodded sagely. 'Ghostcatcher are getting faster.'

Nedly eyed the tarts and sat on his hands. 'That house was empty – I'm sure of it. Who do you think called it in?'

'Someone squawked.' Lil narrowed her eyes at Abe. 'Did you tell anyone you were going there?'

Abe tipped his hat back and fastened his multi-purpose pliers round the handle of his coffee cup. 'Not a soul.'

'Well, they got wind of it from somewhere. If we hadn't picked them up on Quake's scanner, we would never have made it in time.'

'Maybe nobody told them.' Abe scooped up a tart and bit into the flaky pastry, sending a shower of it down his tie to nestle in the pouch of his buttoned jacket. 'They probably just got lucky.'

Lil wasn't convinced. 'They get their tip-offs

from the Haunting Hotline. They weren't just passing; either someone knew where Nedly would be or else that house wasn't really empty.' She took a big gulp of hot chocolate and then licked away the foam moustache. 'What were you doing there anyway?'

Abe gave her a grim look. 'This was delivered this morning.' He pulled a waxy-looking note from his inside pocket, unfolded and flattened it and then slid it across the table to Lil.

It was a copy of a shipping note for a delivery that had come in two days earlier through Peligan City Docks. The vessel was the *Mio Amore*, the description of the goods was simply 'cleaning products', imported by a company called GCI Services, and their delivery address was the one in Chinatown. There was a note clipped to it:

DEAR MANDREL INVESTIGATIONS
THIS CONCERNS YOU.

It was signed simply:

A FRIEND

Nedly pointed. 'That delivery address was the empty old house.'

Lil narrowed her eyes. 'Could have been a set-up. My bet is that this "A Friend" is probably not *a friend* at all. Maybe someone lured you to Chinatown to catch Nedly?'

Nedly's eyes grew as dark and as cold as a deep riverbed.

Abe shifted uncomfortably. 'Maybe we need to start picking our cases more carefully. Anyway, we're not going to be able to work out who they are from this.' He started to fold the note away again but Lil slapped a hand across it, pulled it to her side of the table and gave it the Penetrating Squint.

It was typed in large and urgent-looking capitals, on ordinary paper with no distinguishing marks. 'I wonder what kind of typewriter they used. Did anyone see it being posted? Did it go into your mailbox or under the door?

Abe held up a pastry-crumb-covered finger while he swallowed the mouthful he had just taken and then said, 'Hold on, one thing at a time.' He patted down his mac in search of his notebook.

Lil continued, 'Can you check it for dabs?'

'Dabs? Sure.' He shrugged. 'I can dust it but I've got nothing to check the fingerprints against.'

'Maybe Monbatsu could help?' Lil persisted.

Abe wrinkled his eyes, and scribbled down a few notes. He was beaten but not sorry about it. 'All right, I'll follow it up.'

Nedly pointed at the delivery note. 'I think we should look further into this shipment too, just in case there is something in it.'

'Good idea, Nedly,' said Lil, taking out an old chewed pencil and spinning it a couple of times between her fingers. 'We do need to get the skinny on the cargo but without ruffling any feathers. You check it out, but not on your own. Wherever it leads I'm coming too. If Ghostcatcher comes after you, they're going to have to go through me first.'

'And me,' said Abe.

Margaret barked sharply.

Nedly gave them a crooked smile. 'OK.'

Lil stuck the pencil in her mouth, bit down on it thoughtfully and then said, 'Abe, do you have any contacts down at the harbourmaster's office? If we can find out what the shipment is – if it even exists – who it's for and where it's really going, it would be a start. '

Abe took a last swig of his coffee and put down the empty cup. 'I can do that. Meet me on the corner of Fig Street tomorrow at eleven a.m.' He put on his hat, swiped the newspaper off the table with his pliers and tucked it into his jacket, and then tried a reassuring smile on for size.

Lil returned it gratefully, but when she looked past him out of the window and across the street at the newspaper A-board, her smile dropped. The agent was changing the paper.

The headline was: 'Gordian Vows: the Final Ghost's Days Are Numbered'. Nedly caught her frowning at it and she rolled her eyes breezily as if to say, 'Call that news!'

Abe followed Lil's stare. He shook his head wearily and counted out the last of his change and laid it on the table. 'You would think there was no other news in town.' He shrugged on his coat, and made for the door with Margaret at his heels.

He was right. It was all the *Herald* could talk about. Ghost fever had struck and under its new editor Sam Tangiers the newspaper had recruited extra reporters just to dig for details on the Final Ghost.

The headlines had come thick and fast: *Fright Night at the Spookermarket! Bus Routes Cancelled: Hauntings on the Line! Bank Robber Confesses: the Final Ghost Made Me Do It!*

Every edition, every page. Suddenly, everything was the Final Ghost's fault.

Nedly glared at the A-board in silence, and when he finally spoke his voice was croaky and bitter. 'No matter what I do, no matter how much I try to help fix things, it's not enough. They won't give me a chance.' His bottom lip trembled and he bit down hard to stop it.

Lil mentally kicked her own feelings of despair to the kerb and told him, 'Don't sweat it, Nedly. No one reads the *Herald* anyway.'

But the truth was people *were* reading it. The Final Ghost campaign had been the *Herald*'s most successful yet: circulation figures had tripled. Previously you couldn't have given it away; now people were actually queuing up to buy it.

Even big stories got lost. Weeks earlier Lil had handed the *Klaxon* everything it needed to put two and two together to expose the evil genius Cornelius Gallows. Gallows had bound the spirits of the prisoners from the Secure Wing for the Criminally Insane to a collection of creepy poppets and used them to control the ghosts in an attempt to take over the city, but now he was dead.

No one knew how Gallows had met his end.

It was officially recorded that he was the last victim of the prison epidemic. But the crew of Mandrel Investigations knew there had been no epidemic, and their contact, Monbatsu, a pathologist at the city morgue, told them that Gallows had been strangled. The only known facts were these: Mr Grip, aka the spirit of the Peligan City Strangler, Loid Grainne, was freed by someone, and Gallows, his master, was found, strangled. Perhaps the crimes were linked.

No one would ever know now because the *Herald*, the mouthpiece for City Hall, had buried the results of the inquest and ignored the *Klaxon*'s exposé on Gallows. Lil was certain that as they had reported that Gallows had perished at the asylum more than a decade earlier, they would never admit that they had wrongly recorded his death.

And once the *Herald* realised the newspaper-selling power of ghosts it had jumped wholeheartedly on the bandwagon. The message was simple: ghosts exist, they are a threat, but

City Hall was taking care of them. So what if in order to do this they had to raise taxes and cut back on services? It was all in the interests of public safety.

City Hall's initiative to dispose of the ghosts was an outfit called Ghostcatcher Inc., who had burst onto the scene a few weeks earlier and eliminated the most dangerous ghost of all, Mr Grip, with their high-tech experimental equipment.

Since that night the Ghostcatcher van had been patrolling the streets, but they were only hunting one spook now. They called it the Final Ghost and to Peligan City it was public enemy number one. But Lil and Abe knew the city had it all wrong. The ghost was their friend and his name was Nedly Stubbs.

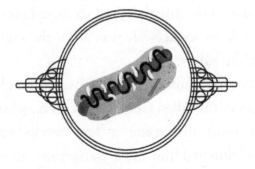

Chapter 3

The Most Important
Meals of the Day

Lil tore up the morning edition of the *Herald* as soon as it landed on the mat and stuffed it into the bag where they kept the bedding for her hamster, Waldo.

In the kitchen the kettle was coming to the boil, the radio was on and the colander of blueberries resting on the draining board meant one thing: pancakes.

'Morning!' Lil said to her mum, and to

Nedly who was sitting on the counter beside the sink.

'Morning!' they both replied at the same time.

'Sleep well?' said Naomi, pushing her spectacles back up her nose.

'Like a log.' Lil poured herself a tall glass of milk and drank half of it straight down.

'Snug as a bug in a rug,' said Nedly, his gaze following Naomi around the room.

Naomi Potkin didn't believe in ghosts. She was one of only two people that Lil knew of who was completely immune to the cold spots and creeping feelings of dread that surrounded Nedly. This made it easier for him to be around at home, and in Naomi's company he could feel more like the boy that he was rather than the ghost he had become, even though she was completely oblivious to his presence. Lil knew she would have to try to convince her mother about Nedly's existence one day; she was just waiting for the right time, but it never seemed to come.

'So, how did you get on last night?' Naomi

put the frying pan on the hob and turned on the heat. 'Have Ghostcatcher come up with anything yet?'

Lil spooned coffee into the pot. 'Nothing but false alarms so far.'

Naomi frowned. 'Gordian should pull the funding before it bankrupts the city.' She threw a handful of blueberries into the mixing bowl. 'If it wasn't for Tangiers stoking the fire every time it died out, people might have forgotten about the Final Ghost; there's so little credible evidence for it now.' She took out her frustration on the batter. Then she turned to the pan and did a double take. 'Did you put the butter in there or did I?'

Lil was confused for a second. 'No. I –' She looked at Nedly, who was standing beside the butter dish beaming proudly. 'Yes – I did it just now.'

Naomi looked across the room to where Lil was standing by the coffee pot and then to the butter bubbling away on the hob in front of her. 'OK, well – thanks.' She ladled the mix into the pan in three golden discs, which expanded until they joined up with each other, like a cloverleaf. 'If only there was some way to prove it.'

Lil turned the radio up a notch and then nodded Nedly over to the kitchen dresser and started rattling the knives and forks in the drawer. 'You can't help, OK – not when Mum's here,' she whispered. 'She doesn't understand.'

Nedly looked down. 'I'm sorry.' The room became colder, the steam that rose from the coffee cups turned white, and the grey morning light darkened. Naomi flipped the pancakes out of the pan and squinted out of the window at the clouds.

Lil tried to catch Nedly's eye. 'It's not your fault; it's just –' She jumped as Naomi put the plate on the table with a clonk, and grabbed a handful of cutlery.

'Anyway,' Naomi continued, 'you're the one with front-row seats as far as Ghostcatcher is concerned. Do *you* think there's anything in it?'

Lil carefully placed the knives and forks on

the table. 'The Final Ghost?' Nedly was standing right in front of her; she tried not to look at him. 'I think . . . I think I'm just going to keep an open mind for now.'

'That's the best kind to have.' Naomi kissed her on the forehead and walked through Nedly, who cringed at the contact and turned a sickly shade of grey.

Lil sat at the table and pulled out a second chair, angled slightly towards hers for Nedly to collapse into, putting her feet on the rungs so it didn't look suspicious, then squeezed the maple syrup over her pancakes in a whirl, considered them for a second, and then squeezed again and went back the other way.

Naomi made another three pancakes for herself and then picked up a fork in one hand and her plate in the other and ate them leaning against the counter.

'How about you?' said Lil. 'What are you working on?'

'Something's going on out at Bun Hill, at the orphanage there.'

Lil and Nedly exchanged alarmed glances.

'The Hawks Memorial Orphanage! I know it,' said Lil. Nedly had lived there all his life. 'What do they say?'

'It sounds like someone has poisoned their garden. All the winter vegetables have perished and all the grass around it, right down to the road.'

'No!' said Lil. 'Who would have done that?'

'Well, I'm not jumping to any conclusions. It might just be a natural occurrence. The land gets worked pretty hard out there. The caretaker –' she pulled her notebook out of her back pocket and flipped through it – 'Mr Kolchak, says there's something in the soil. Could be some kind of disease but maybe it's something else. I'll see if I can get a sample tested. If it's suspicious, then we can run a story on it. If we exert some pressure on City Hall, maybe they'll investigate.' She sounded doubtful.

The pancakes weighed heavily in Lil's belly. 'Have the orphans got enough to eat?'

'We should check it out,' Nedly urged her.

'People are dropping off food when they can spare it. They've got enough in storage to get them through the rest of winter but if whatever it is in the soil is still causing trouble come spring, things will be tough.'

'I know some of the folk up there. I'd like to help.'

Naomi's face brightened. 'If nothing much is brewing with Ghostcatcher, why not talk to Logan, see if you can get a swap? It would be nice to work together on something.'

Lil stared at her empty plate. Working on a story with her mother was her dream, but Lil didn't speak until she could trust herself to give the right answer, not the one she wanted to give. Out of the corner of her eye she could see Nedly nodding encouragingly, but Lil shook her head. 'No, I think I better stick with Ghostcatcher for now. I want to stay on it, see it through.'

Nedly sighed.

'But keep me posted, OK?' she added.

'No problem.' Naomi put the plate down,

gave Lil a quick smile, picked up the coffee and drank it quickly. She winced. 'Eurgh! This is lukewarm! So, do you want to tag along to the orphanage after work anyway?'

'Yes,' said Nedly.

'I can't,' Lil insisted. 'I've got something on.'

'Are you seeing the mysterious Nedly?'

Lil hesitated and then said, 'Yep.'

Naomi pushed the last bite of pancake around the plate, trying to chase it onto the fork. 'I'm still waiting to meet him.'

Nedly turned his bushbaby eyes on Lil.

'You will. You definitely will. I promise.' Nedly blinked hopefully at her and she gulped. 'At some point.' He flickered and then wilted like a leaky balloon, sinking through the kitchen chair until he was sitting half buried in the lino. Lil's heart sank with him.

'OK.' Naomi gave her a curious look. 'Well, I'll look forward to it.'

By late morning a haze of smog hung over Peligan City. Lil, Nedly, Abe and Margaret approached the hot dog cart, stepping through the steam coming off the grill.

Abe tipped his hat. 'How's it going, Minnie?'

Minnie returned the greeting with a crooked smile. 'Same as always, detective. What can I get you?' Her freckled face was surrounded by the hood of her anorak, which she had zipped right up over her jacket and cloth money belt. She had strung her greasy apron round it all and wiped her hands there before she picked up the bag of finger rolls.

Abe shuffled further under the canopy of the cart. 'I'll take one with the works as usual. Lil?'

Lil eyed up the sausages that were rolling back and forth under Minnie's slice, trying to weigh up whether she could physically fit a hot dog in her pancake-stuffed belly, while the sweet smell of frying onions suggested that she should give it a go. 'I'm not sure . . .' she stalled.

Abe cut in. 'It's my treat.' And he got out a couple of notes from his wallet to show he meant business.

Minnie nodded approvingly. 'Gumshoe work finally paying off, detective?'

'I can't complain.' Abe shrugged as he yanked the prosthetic hand off with a pop and pulled out the hot dog holder attachment, ready to take delivery.

'It's about time your luck changed.'

Nedly was looking from the grill to Margaret, who was sitting bolt upright on the pavement, shivering slightly in the rain.

'Don't even think about it,' Lil murmured to him. 'She can have a bit of mine.'

Margaret cocked her head to one side, her soulful eyes staying with Nedly; they told him 'a bit' wouldn't do it.

'I'll take one with onions, ketchup. And a splash of mustard,' Lil added daringly. She was building up to the works.

Minnie winked. 'My personal favourite combination.' She handed Abe his bun laden with everything it was possible to put on a hot dog and paused over Margaret who locked in with glistening, hopeful eyes.

'Don't let her put the squeeze on you,' Abe insisted.

'Sorry, pal,' Minnie sighed down to Margaret. 'If you were my dog, I'd give you a sausage, but it looks like you got landed with old heart-of-stone here. Not your fault but that's how it is. Here's your change, detective.' She held it out to him and he spread his hand under hers ready to take it. They stood there like that for a long moment, and then Minnie asked him: 'Is that a new hat you're wearing?'

Abe narrowed his eyes. 'The brim peeled off the other one. It got melted, remember?'

Minnie nodded. 'Goes really well with that new tie. Grasshoppers,' she said admiringly. 'Very nice. Feels good to spoil yourself once in a while, eh?'

'All right, all right.' Abe clenched his jaw and withdrew his hand. 'You win. Give me a third dog, for the dog.'

'Coming right up!' Minnie grinned and threw the change into her money belt and started browning up a sausage.

Abe looked down at Margaret as if to say, *Satisfied?* Margaret looked defiantly back at him.

Nedly beamed. 'I'll do the honours.'

Minnie chewed her gum and flipped the onions a couple of times. 'It's like I always say, what's the use of money if you don't spend it?'

'You really have got big ears.' Abe gave Minnie a reproving look. 'I just had a couple of cases go my way, that's all.'

'Heard you're getting quite a rep again. Back to like how things were when you helped clean up this town,' she persisted.

Abe gave her a bashful shrug. 'I do OK.'

'Carry on like this and I bet the Squad will want you back on the books. Only matter of time, I reckon.' She flashed him a yellow-toothed smile. 'That's just what I heard.'

Abe basked in the glow for a while but then the cold stare Lil gave him chilled it. 'I've had some help,' he confessed.

'Yeah, I heard that too.' Minnie winked at Lil and then blew a small bubble and popped it. 'Whoever it is, they must be pretty handy to pull Mandrel Investigations out of skid row.'

It was Nedly's turn to look bashful and Lil grinned at him.

'Tell me something I don't know,' Abe replied gruffly. 'Like, about a mysterious shipment coming in through Peligan City docks a couple of nights ago.'

Minnie's expression grew serious; she leant forward and murmured through tight lips, 'One of many.'

'Know what's in it?'

Minnie shrugged. 'They're shifting some kind of specialised material in large quantities. My money is on a smuggling op, organised crime, but word on the street is it's legit.'

'If it's legit, why all the intrigue?' Lil took the pencil out of her hair and tapped it against her nose. 'The delivery address was a dummy and they brought it in under the cover of night.'

'Beats me,' said Minnie.

Lil took the sausage for Margaret, then crouched down behind the cart. Nedly knelt beside her and stared intently at his hand until it started to glow fiercely. Then he laid it out flat and Lil tipped the sausage into his palm. Nedly carefully rolled it to the end of his fingers and offered it to Margaret, who proudly sat down to accept the reward like a small furry lord waiting to be knighted.

Abe took a bite out of his hot dog and chewed it thoughtfully. 'Any idea when the next one will be?'

'Tonight. 11.55 p.m.'

Lil clambered back to her feet. 'Don't suppose you know which dock?'

'The one by pier seven.'

Nedly was transfixed by the sight of Margaret chomping on the sausage like a fat cigar. 'Lil!' he cried gleefully. 'Look at how she's eating it.' He stepped closer to watch.

Minnie shuddered suddenly and dropped the scoop of onions. 'Sorry.' Her hand was shaking as she picked it up again. 'Can't help feeling on edge with the Final Ghost still on the loose.' She looked over her shoulder. 'The whole town is spooked. No one knows when it's going to strike – not even me, and I know pretty much everything.'

Nedly backed away, embarrassed.

'Maybe he's not going to strike at all – maybe he's gone,' Lil ventured.

Minnie didn't look convinced. 'Then why does it still feel so creepy?' She shivered and then Abe shivered.

'I don't feel creepy,' he insisted. 'It's in your head. You better stop reading the *Herald*; it's giving you ideas.'

'Ha!' Minnie chuckled drily. 'Don't insult me! I've been keeping my ears open, that's all, and word on the street is the Final Ghost is just biding its time.' She shook the mustard bottle expertly, whiplashing her wrist to get the last of it to the top. 'That's why the Ghostcatcher van is out patrolling the streets every night. Word is they're getting close too. Let's hope they get it – and soon.'

Nedly's face grew stretched and thin-looking. He wrung one hand with the other and stared over his shoulder, scanning the road behind him and then turned quickly to Lil. 'I better go. I'll see you later. I've got some stuff to do.'

'No, wait – !' Lil started, but she was too late. He ran away from them, across the road, barely breaking his stride as he ploughed through the line of taxis that swerved to a stop when they felt the sudden wave of fright. The drivers pressed down their horns and shouted at each other until the creeps wore off, while Nedly vanished into the rain.

Margaret dropped her ears and whined.

When Lil looked back Minnie was still paused with the mustard bottle poised above the bun and a quizzical expression on her face. 'I've . . . I've changed my mind, about the mustard,' Lil faltered. 'I'll just have ketchup.'

Minnie returned the mustard to the cart and then handed over the hot dog. She looked all around her and then shoved her hands in her pockets and shrugged her shoulders a few times to shake the cold out of them. 'It's weird; this spooky feeling just comes and goes. The air felt thick with creepiness a couple of minutes ago but I don't feel it now – now everything feels OK.'

'Actually,' Lil murmured, looking dismally at Abe. 'I don't think it does.'

Chapter 4

The Docks

At a quarter to midnight the docks were quiet except for the clanking of rigging. The air smelt salty and slightly rotten. In between the warehouses hurricane lamps pooled light onto the quayside, a strip of concrete that ended where the black, glittering water began.

Further inland on higher ground, Lil was crouched behind an old wagon just beyond a disused railway siding. She stifled a yawn and stared out at the sheeting rain from beneath the hood of her yellow mac. 'Is it nearly time yet?' Her cold fingers gripped the edge of the wagon as she peered over it.

'We've still got a few minutes.' Abe winced as he tried to straighten his legs a little without standing up and breaking cover. 'Any sign of the kid?'

'Not yet.' Lil sighed. She tried to stretch the unyielding fabric of her mac further over her knees to keep the rain off her jeans. 'But he'll be here. He said he would be. Any time now.' Margaret gave a doleful whine from her shelter under the wagon.

'I don't doubt it.' Abe cranked out a smile. He wiped the rain out of his eyes with a wet sleeve, pulled off his rubber hand and stuffed it into his mac pocket and then browsed the attachments of his Swiss Army hand and selected a miniature vice. 'It's a tough break. He must feel like the whole city wants him –' Abe's gaze dropped to his soaked and battered shoes – 'gone.'

Lil kept her eyes on the water. 'He can't help being . . . not alive.'

'No argument here. I'd change things for him if I could.' Abe cleared his throat gruffly and pulled a pair of binoculars out of his other pocket. Lil glanced across to see him tighten the vice round them and fiddle with the focus wheel. 'Unfortunately,' he continued, 'as long as everyone – and by everyone I mean the *Herald* – is worrying about the Final Ghost –'

Lil interrupted pointing at the binoculars. 'They're new.'

Abe stretched the fingers of his left hand protectively over the casing. 'I thought they might come in handy. For stake-outs,' he added, training them on a red-and-white striped buoy bobbing in the black water, and then tracked across to pier seven. 'What I'm saying is, it's a distraction; while the Final Ghost is making headlines no one is paying attention to all the other stuff that's happening, like who's been poisoning the orphanage garden.'

Lil gave him the Squint. 'How do you know about that?'

Abe shrugged his collar up round his neck and sank his chin into it. 'Naomi must have mentioned it. She knew that I'd done some work for the old guy so . . .' He changed the subject quickly. 'I mean, the Golden Loop should be bringing in millions in taxes for the city: where is it all going?'

'Mum's always saying that too.'

Abe pulled an already damp handkerchief out of his pocket and wiped the rain off his face, scattering fluff to the wind. 'Well, she makes a lot of sense.'

There was a sound like the lid being turned on a fizzy drink, but only Lil heard it.

Abe went back to staring through the binoculars. 'You know, I've never been a popular guy –' he paused for Lil to contradict him and then when she said nothing frowned a little and continued – 'but it must be tough knowing that you give people the creeps – ow!' He adjusted his position. 'People just don't understand. To them he's just another murderous spook. Ow!' He winced painfully. 'Like something out of a nightmare. OW! Do you realise that's my toe you keep standing on?' He caught Lil's glare and returned it with a rueful one that said, *He's here, isn't he?* Abe swallowed hard and then cleared his throat. 'Hey. Good to have you back, kid.'

Nedly shrugged. He looked bone-tired. His eyes were dull, with the sheen of a dirty window, and his skin had a hazy quality.

'You OK?' Lil furrowed her brows at him. 'You don't look too good.'

'Thanks!' He smiled weakly and then looked past her at the water. Lil watched his face in profile, the docks visible through his cheek.

'Is that the one?' Nedly pointed and Lil pulled her eyes away.

'Here she comes!' Abe cried.

A boat rolled in across the water, a shadow strung with dimmed lamps. It pulled along the quayside, churning water, and then cut its engines and drifted into place in silence. Thick ropes were flung out and a gang of stevedores in plaid jackets and wool caps emerged from the warehouse to catch them and pull the boat into dock against the rubber tyres that lined the quay.

Abe adjusted his focus as the lights reached the prow of the boat. 'The *Amore Mio*,' he breathed.

Nedly leant over between them, sending a shiver down Lil's spine and making Abe shudder so hard that he hit himself on the nose with the binoculars. His eyes filled with tears.

'Sorry!' Nedly pulled away. 'Will you tell him?' he asked Lil.

'Nedly says he's sorry, if he gave you the creeps just then.'

'It's not you, kid.' Abe squeezed his eyelids dry with a finger and thumb. 'It's this infernal wind and rain. You sit tight with us.' He held the binoculars back to his eyes with a trembling hand.

Lil smiled gratefully and then whispered to Nedly. 'I'm glad you're here.'

'Where else would I be?' murmured Abe.

They could hear instructions being yelled from the dockside as the arm of the gantry crane arched out over the ship, swinging a heavy chain beneath it.

Lil could only just make out the action below; the stevedores looked no bigger than matchsticks to her naked eye. 'What's happening now?'

'They're getting ready to unload,' Abe replied. The chain had disappeared into the hold and after a few moments a winch began raising the cargo. It was a pallet stacked with smaller wooden crates, like tea chests.

A truck pulled onto the loading dock and then reversed in a semicircle towards the ship.

Abe adjusted the focus to read the number plate. 'That truck is one of the city fleet.'

Lil eyed his binoculars enviously. 'Stolen?'

Abe shrugged and turned the focus wheel again. 'Maybe.'

'Look!' A couple of darkly dressed matchsticks

had entered the scene. 'Security guards?' Lil guessed.

Abe set his jaw grimly. 'Police. Whatever they're doing it's official business. *City* business by the look of it.'

The two police officers stood aside while stevedores started unloading, hauling the crates down from the ship on pulleys and swinging them over to the dockside and onto the base of the truck with no more sound than the rattling of rusty chains.

'What's happening now?'

'Nothing much; they're still unloading.'

'Well, then can I borrow the binoculars?' Lil persisted.

Abe took the binoculars away from his eyes for a moment to give her a wary look. 'I'm using them.'

Lil pursed her lips at Abe. 'You said nothing much was happening.'

He carried on looking defiantly into the lenses.

'I only want to look through for a second.'

'I'll tell you if I see anything important.'

'Just for a second.'

'It would take too long for me to let go of them.'

'Fine.' Lil paused and then added, 'Now what's happening?'

Abe gave a bull-like snort and clenched his jaw. He painstakingly unscrewed the small vice that held the binoculars and offered them to Lil. 'Two minutes, and then I'm taking them back.' Lil took hold of one side but Abe didn't let go of the other. 'And I want to know exactly what you see.'

'Fine. I don't know why you're making such a big deal of it. They're only binoculars.'

'*My* binoculars,' Abe corrected her.

Lil refocused them and scanned to the left where a smart black Austin Cambridge had pulled up. 'There's another car.'

A single man got out, wearing a grey felt homburg with the brim pulled down low and a dark wool overcoat. Lil squinted through the lens. 'Looks like an official someone. He's talking to one of the dockers; he's showing him a clipboard.' She dipped the binoculars. 'Maybe he's the harbourmaster?'

Abe held his hand out. 'Let me see.'

'I still have a minute and a half.'

'Hand them over.' Abe held out his hand again. Reluctantly Lil handed them over.

Abe spent a minute retightening the vice round the binoculars so that he could lift them and then another minute groaning about how hard it was to get the focus back.

They watched as a man in a chequered wool cap approached the man in the suit. The two men stood and talked beneath one of the white dock lights, where the mist from the river was picked out like a cone of swirling light.

Abe touched the focus wheel again. 'I'll bet the chequered cap is the head stevedore. The guy in the suit looks like the buyer come to check on the goods.'

Lil looked at Nedly and nodded to one side. He looked back and shook his head. Lil nodded hers again, more firmly this time. A dangerous gleam came into her eye.

Abe continued, 'Now the suit is asking the cap a question and the cap is shrugging and the suit is looking at his watch. Now he's holding out his hand for the paperwork.'

The suit finished reading through the papers on the clipboard and then pointed at one of the crates. The head stevedore disappeared from view and then returned with a menacing-looking crowbar.

'What the . . . ?' Abe let the binoculars drop an inch and then he refocused them quickly and breathed out a sigh of relief. The stevedore was levering open the lid of one of the crates. 'I thought we were going to witness a murder! OK, so he's levering open one of the crates and the suit is putting on a white glove and then he's reaching in and pulling out a small cloth bag and tipping the contents into his palm. It looks like . . . little chips of coal? I don't know what that is.' He paused; something yellow flitted across the foreground of his field of vision.

Abe caught his breath, let the binoculars drop from his eyes and then quickly picked them up again and scanned across until he picked up Lil, crouch-running down to the warehouse.

He shook his head despairingly, ground his teeth and then muttered, 'Looks like it's just me and you now, kid.' He paused for a deep sigh. 'Maybe you should go down there and keep an eye on her. If needs be, we can cause a distraction.' He looked down at an old discarded chocolate wrapper. 'If you agree, move that wrapper to the left.' The wrapper remained caught in the grass. 'If you disagree, move it to the right.' No movement.

'He's gone too, hasn't he? How do you like that?' He paused, checked the view through the binoculars again and then took his eyes away to look down at Margaret. The space under the wagon was empty. Abe shook his head wearily and went back to the binoculars. 'I'm just talking to myself.'

* * *

Down on the dockside, Lil peered round the side of the warehouse. The bitumen-stained doors were warped by the salt in the air and instead of lying flat they curved enough to cast a shadow for her to hide in.

Nedly stood opposite her. They were close enough to the *Amore Mio* to see the frothy yellow scum that carpeted the water round her prow, along with rubbish and an oil spill that reflected a rainbow.

The man in the suit had pulled out what looked like a jeweller's eyeglass and was peering at the lumps of coal with it. Lil gave Nedly a shrug that meant, *What is that stuff?* and then rolled her eyes towards it in a way that meant, *Can you get a closer look at the label on the bag?*

Nedly nodded confidently. 'I'm on it!'

Lil watched him jog to the front of the warehouse and then step out onto the quayside and walk up to the man in the suit. He was rolling the coal back into the bag and sealing it. Nedly craned, ducked and dived round him trying to read what was written there. The suit got spooked and started darting looks all around. He threw the bag back into the crate and Nedly plunged his head in after. Lil shuddered as the lid was closed on him; it looked like a bad beheading.

The suit shouted at the head stevedore and he sprang into action, hammering the lid back on the crate. Nedly extricated himself from it and queasily staggered back towards the man in the suit who was scribbling things on the clipboard. As Nedly moved in to see what was written there the suit looked up suddenly and shivered. He whipped his head round and then barked at everyone to get a move on, his eyes nervously scanning the darkness beyond the dockside.

The stevedore looked haggard and edgy, like he would rather be anywhere else but there. The man in the suit finished writing, tore off the top sheet and then slapped the clipboard against the stevedore's stomach by way of passing it to him. Clutching his own copy of the paperwork he strode off towards the warehouse with Nedly running alongside him, head bent to one side, still trying to see what was written there.

Lil pinned herself more closely to the wall. She breathed in and held it. The man in the suit stopped suddenly, and then took another slower step forward. Lil slunk backwards as quickly as she could, but stepped on a twig, which snapped. She froze.

A sharp bark cut through the air. The suit pulled out a torch and shone it across the embankment. He stared out at its beam for a minute and then jerked his thumb impatiently at the waiting truck driver who jumped into the cab. A tarpaulin was rolled out over the back of the truck, the sides were bolted up and the cargo was tied down. The engine sputtered into life.

Lil tried to trickle her breath out nice and slowly. Nedly flew round the side of the warehouse to join her and Margaret scampered down the path towards them from the other side. Lil bent down to give her a grateful rub on the head and straightened quickly again as headlights burst across the darkness and trawled the scrub ahead of them. As the truck backed up Lil made a note of the number plate. They waited until the red tail lights were far enough away, then they all ran after it.

Chapter 5

A Familiar Road

'Come on!' Lil urged Abe when they reached the wagon. 'The truck is leaving!'

Abe had only been able to crank himself to half-bent knees. 'Don't wait for me!' he gasped.

Lil nodded quickly and then, keeping low, sprinted up the hill and over the wasteland to the lane where the Zodiac was parked. She swung open the passenger door with the busted lock and shot into the seat, Nedly nosedived expertly through the closed back window and landed behind her and Margaret leapt onto Lil's lap. Lil clicked her seat belt in. Then they waited.

From the track that led to the docks two cylinders of light appeared, blinking once at a bend, then growing larger. They heard the crackle of gravel under wheels as the headlights neared, skimming the verges like a trawl net. Lil ducked down as it passed and then all three turned to see the hulking shadow of Abe lumbering over the ridge towards them. The truck lights illuminated the junction at the end of the lane just as he reached the Zodiac and flumped down behind the wheel to catch his breath.

Lil held the ignition key out to him in readiness while Abe turned the tiny screw that loosened the vice round the binoculars as quickly as he could. Lil bored her eyes into it but it didn't get any looser any faster.

'Can't you – ?' she started.

'Don't say it!' He shook his head at her and carried on twiddling until finally the binoculars came loose.

Lil drummed her feet on the footwell as Abe selected his driving attachment and accepted the key Lil offered him. She sat on her hands and stared pointedly ahead but couldn't resist a mumble through gritted teeth that sounded a lot like *finally!* when he got the engine running.

The Zodiac strained into life and swung out of the track, wheels churning mud and throwing up gravel. They hurtled down the lane, bouncing off the verges like a giant turquoise pinball. Abe winced as the car juddered over a pothole but he kept his foot on the accelerator. As soon as they were close enough to use the truck's tail lights to navigate by, he dropped his speed and killed the Zodiac's headlights, and they became a shadow, prowling from a safe distance behind.

To their left Peligan City twinkled at them, buildings spiking the horizon like the teeth of a broken comb. As they passed the winged roofs of the mansions of Yang Guang Heights, Lil realised that they were not heading back into town at all; they were skirting the outer limits to the north.

'Nedly, what did the address on the delivery form say this time?'

'The same as the last one, the house in Chinatown.'

Lil looked out of the window as the lights receded. They turned west, splashing through the puddles on the narrow lanes, until at last they came to a road that she recognised. Bun Hill.

Up ahead the Hawks Memorial Orphanage was mostly in darkness apart from a few windows that glowed warmly through bright patterned curtains.

Lil raised her eyebrows as she looked back at Nedly. His interested expression quickly turned grave and pinched-looking as a ruined silhouette appeared on the hill opposite.

'The old asylum,' he murmured.

Abe slowed the Zodiac right down as they followed the truck along the eerily familiar track, under the arched canopy of crooked trees with branches that dangled like gnarled fingers. The car's suspension groaned and the bunch of coconuts that hung from the rear-view mirror swayed uneasily.

The truck stopped in front of the metal gates. Someone had added a row of red lights beneath the sign, illuminating the words 'Rorschach Asylum' and making them look demonic.

'Now what?' Abe cut the engine, and they sat there, steam coming off the bonnet.

The driver jumped down from the cab, turning her collar up to the rain. At the gate she opened a small cabinet that was fixed to the right-hand post, picked up a telephone receiver and said something into it. There was a low warning buzzer and suddenly the lights turned an eerie green. The driver climbed back into her cab and with a shunting sound the gates swung open by themselves and the truck drove in. The gates closed quickly behind her and the light switched back to red.

'That's new,' Lil whispered.

They left the Zodiac parked up by the

undergrowth and headed forward on foot. Lil and Abe arched their torch beams over the new set-up. The rusty iron gates had been upgraded to steel ones but the 'Keep Out' and 'Danger' signs were still there.

Abe and Lil knew Rorschach Asylum from their first case together; it was where Cornelius Gallows had holed up after he faked his own death, executed Leonard Owl and created his first weaponised ghost, Mr Glimmer. Abe and Lil had both nearly died in the fire that Mr Glimmer had set, but there had been enough of the spirit of Owl left within Mr Glimmer to lead them to safety before freeing himself from Gallows' clutches.

To Nedly the asylum would always be the worst spot on earth: the place where his short life had ended. He glanced fearfully at it, his pale skin dull and filmy, his eyes dark and saucer-shaped.

'Looks like they don't like uninvited guests.' Abe nodded at the telephone handset. 'I wonder who picks this up at the other end.'

Beside the gates the old chain-link perimeter fence had been replaced too, with three metre high railings, spiked iron poles only a few centimetres apart.

Lil measured up to them. 'We're not getting through there.'

She stared despondently past the gates at what was left of Rorschach Asylum. Twice-burned, the roofless ruin was jagged against the sky, blackened and rain-soaked, looking every bit the haunted house it had once been.

'There can't be much of it left now after that last fire.' Abe eyed it grimly.

Lil studied the pearly light emanating from behind the dark silhouette. 'There has to be something there. Is that moonlight or . . .' She looked up – no, the moon was elsewhere.

Nedly hung back. 'We should check it out . . . at the library.'

Lil knew he didn't want to go in, but she couldn't pull her eyes away from the intriguing ghostly halo behind the ruins. 'Let's just have a quick poke around while we're here. It might be nothing.'

Nedly gave her a complicated look. They both knew that it definitely wouldn't be nothing.

Abe frowned at the fence. 'It's a lot of security for an old dump like this.' He scratched under his hat with his driving attachment. 'These bars are high; the gaps between them are narrow. The way I see it, there's no way in, unless we can get them to open that gate for us . . .' He ran out of steam as Margaret appeared suddenly on the other side of the fence, bathed in the glow of the red lights.

'She went under it,' said Nedly. 'There's a gap.'

Lil crouched down to examine the space and frowned. 'It's too small for me.'

Abe rubbed his chin appraisingly. 'Me too.' He looked confidently but wrongly at the area between himself and Lil. 'Nedly, how about you check it out?'

Lil read the look on Nedly's face. 'I don't think that's such a good idea – it's getting late.'

Confusion crossed Abe's face. 'I thought you said –' Then he caught her eye and saw her head give a minute shake. He nodded grimly. 'We'll think of another way. There might not be anything in it anyway.'

Nedly sighed deeply. 'OK, I'll go.'

'You really don't have to,' Lil told him.

'I know. But we're here now. I'm just going to see what that glow is, then I'll come back. I'm not going inside the building.'

'Fair enough.'

Nedly began wriggling his shoulders. He turned side-on and started to squeeze himself through the railing. No sooner had his arm crossed the boundary than the long grass they were standing in started flickering. Lil looked up to see that the lights over the gate were flashing brightly.

'Nedly,' she warned him. 'Wait a sec.' She turned to Abe. 'What do you think that means?' They all paused to watch the lights.

Lil frowned. 'I've got a bad feeling.'

Abe whistled sharply and Margaret ran back

and shimmied under the fence. They began hurrying back down the lane, Abe's binoculars thumping against his chest.

Lil risked a glance over her shoulder. Torchlights were bouncing along the tangled grass in front of the asylum, winking and disguising whoever was carrying them. 'Looks like we've got company,' she gasped.

They reached the Zodiac and piled in. Abe tried to choke the engine to life.

Nedly stared back at the overgrown lawn of the asylum. 'They do not like trespassers!'

The outline of three figures was visible now, running with difficulty through the long grass, encumbered by their white hazmat suits and orange reflective visors.

'Don't panic!' said Abe. 'We'll just say we took a wrong turn.' He jerked the ignition key again. Nothing happened.

Behind the torch beams another light shone through, something glowing green and winking.

A sudden feeling of danger struck Lil.

'Uh-oh!' she whispered. 'I think I know whose place this is.'

The green laser net sprang out from the winking console and stretched over the dark, tufty lawn.

'Ghostcatcher!' breathed Nedly.

Lil shrieked, 'GO. GO. GO!'

Abe rammed the key round again, but the Zodiac wouldn't go. He swiped the sweat from his forehead with his sleeve, took off the handbrake, and then leapt from the car shouting, 'You drive!'

'What?' Lil was confused but she slid into the seat he had just vacated. Abe planted his hands on the front bumper, put his shoulders into it and started pushing. Lil watched his face grow puce with the effort; she recognised that he was asking her to do something, but couldn't read his lips in between his grimacing and grunting breaths.

Suddenly Nedly yelled, 'Put it in reverse!' It took Lil a few goes to find the right position but she popped it just as the speed of the car outpaced the man pushing it. Abe staggered forward, the car rolling backwards. Lil heard him shout, 'Turn the key!'

She instinctively floored the accelerator and rammed the key clockwise, praying for the engine to turn over. She screwed her eyes shut, felt the Zodiac grumble to life and then opened them to see Abe running desperately after the car as it travelled bumpily backwards.

'Slow down!' Nedly yelled.

Lil took her foot off the pedal and scrambled for the passenger seat as Abe caught up enough to lump in beside her and take over the wheel as he braced his other arm round the seat and the Zodiac charged backwards, reversing out into the road and right into the path of blinding headlights and the blare of a horn. They ploughed up the verge opposite and then screeched to a sliding halt as a lorry streaked by. Abe's hand was trembling as he put the car into first and they crawled out of the long grass and back to the city.

* * *

It was nearly two in the morning when they sputtered on to Angel Lane.

Number ten was in darkness but for a couple of lit windows: the narrow one above the front door and Lil's attic bedroom.

Abe gave her a grim smile as she climbed out of the car and opened the rear door for Nedly. Lil tapped lightly on the car roof and Abe drove away.

Closing the front door as silently as possible, she took off her mac and shoes in the hall. She said goodnight to Nedly at the airing cupboard and he slipped through the door to sleep amongst the warm and freshly laundered sheets, while she climbed up the second staircase. A thin strip of light shone under the door at the top of the landing. Lil trained her eyes on it and took another step. A shadow split the light. She put her hand on the door knob, sucked in a deep breath, and then twisted it. From inside came the faint sound of something being moved and then she swung the door open.

Naomi Potkin was sitting on the bed. She

was wearing her pyjamas and dressing gown and her hands were locked anxiously round her knees.

She looked at Lil from over her spectacles. Her eyes looked a little red and glassy. She said: 'I was worried.'

'Sorry I'm late, Mum,' Lil said as she sat down beside her. 'But I was OK. I was with Abe.'

Naomi took her hand, laced their fingers and kissed it. She sighed. 'Lil, Abe Mandrel is a good man but he's no better at keeping out of trouble than you are.'

Lil bit her lip. She wondered what her mum had been doing before she arrived. How long had she been sitting there? The wall of newspaper clippings was opposite, where Lil tacked all her favourite stories, the picture of A. J. McNair's silhouette in the middle of it. Her dressing table was stacked high with books, detective fiction mostly gleaned from bookshelves around the house. Her wardrobe doors were open but there was nothing in there but clothes.

Naomi gave her hand a squeeze. 'So, what were you up to?'

'You know, just helping him out,' Lil murmured vaguely. Her eyes went down to the floor. There, under the bed the corner of her blue scrapbook was just visible. 'We were investigating something.'

Lil pushed the scrapbook out of sight with the heel of her boot.

'Well, you should probably get some sleep then.' Naomi tucked Lil's hair behind her ears and kissed her on the forehead. Lil saw a tiny crease appear between her mother's eyebrows. She held Lil's head in a nutcracker hug for a second, kissed her again on the top it, and whispered, 'Goodnight.'

Lil waited until her mother's footsteps had reached the first-floor landing and then she quickly peeled off her damp clothes, put on her pyjamas and climbed into bed. She lay there for a moment; her heart still felt as though it was racing so she leant over the edge of her mattress and reached round until she found the corner of the scrapbook and dragged it out from its hiding place. She pulled the covers round her, and by the low light of her bedside lamp opened the scrapbook.

In the centre of the first page was the photograph of the McNair reporters, a hurriedly made photocopy that Lil had taken from the framed picture in the office of the *Klaxon* HQ. The reflection from the glass had darkened it, so it was almost impossible to make out any details, but Lil looked closely at the man with the short beard, whose hair was dark like hers but slightly wavy and parted to one side with a cowlick at the front. His white shirt looked crisp, even though the sleeves were rolled up and the top button was undone. Lil had never known what colour his tie was; it looked dark, maybe blue or red, but there wasn't any pattern on it; it was just plain.

Roland Selznick. Lil tried to imagine what his face would have looked like in real life. Then when she was almost ready to fall asleep she turned to her favourite story and began

reading. It was an exposé on the union racket in the Blue Sky Paint factory, where daring young reporter Selznick had broken his first story by going undercover. Lil read it, even as her eyes were drooping shut, and she fell asleep there, propped up on her pillow with the scrapbook laid out across the bed.

Chapter 6

Long Overdue

The following morning Lil and Nedly left early so that they had plenty of time for research before Lil's volunteer work started. The sun had only just risen and a haze of fine rain floated down from the low clouds.

They took Lil's bike, with Nedly perched on the handlebars, entirely weightless, but even so adding to the chill that was freezing the raindrops clinging to Lil's hair.

'Of all the places,' he said despondently, 'it had to be Rorschach Asylum.'

Lil skidded slightly in a puddle and had to drop one foot and then push off on it to stabilise them. 'I don't like it either.' She frowned. 'But as secret hideouts go it's got form.'

'Do you think they know about Gallows and what he did there?' Nedly shuddered and Lil jerked the handlebars involuntarily. A car horn blared at her.

'I don't think so. It's just land to them, somewhere private.'

'Of all the places,' he said again.

'I know,' said Lil, and swung the bike into the courtyard at the back of the Peligan City Public Library.

She heaved herself up onto the windowsill, clambered through the peeling frame, dropped down onto the toilet cistern on the other side and waited for Nedly to follow suit, holding the window open while he gingerly lowered himself into the cubicle. It would have been so much faster if he just came in through the wall but he still hated passing through solid objects.

Once they were inside the atrium, Lil entered the four-digit code into a keypad at the side of a sturdy door that was signposted 'Reading Room'. They heard the familiar buzz and some metallic clunking and the door swung open.

Lil checked they were alone and then whispered, 'OK, we know what's coming in and we know who wants it. The question now is, why is it so important?'

'And why do they need so much of it?' Nedly walked quickly alongside her. 'The invoice I saw at the docks read: twenty-seven crates, black tourmaline. T.O.U.R.M.A.L.I.N.E.'

'I've never heard of it,' said Lil.

'Me neither, but it looked like some kind of stone. And it was shiny. Maybe it's precious? Maybe we've stumbled on a jewellery smuggling ring?'

Lil raised her eyebrows approvingly. 'Maybe that's how Ghostcatcher are funding their equipment. Selling stolen jewels?' She pulled out a pencil and gave it a good chew. 'That would be a great story. But wouldn't they just hand it straight over to the buyer?' She flicked through the card index file.

Nedly searched the air for answers. 'Maybe they had to polish it first?'

'That's not out of the question.' Lil pulled out a card and studied it. 'Nedly, the newspaper archive isn't going to cut it this time. For the kind of stuff we need we'll have to look up there.' She let her gaze drift upwards to the mezzanine that encircled the domed ceiling. 'In the reference library.'

The reference library was reached by a heavy wooden staircase that cut across the wall in the far corner. The floor was carpeted thickly to absorb the noise of footsteps. An outer ring of shelves with free-standing bays stood at regular intervals, like the hour marks on a clock face. The inner ring, which looked down onto the main library, had strong wooden railings. High-level sloped reading desks were at the end of each bay for customers to rest the huge reference books with spines that were several inches thick. There was a smell of wood polish with a slight undercurrent of mustiness.

Lil crouched down and stared through the railings at the room below. The wheel of shelves radiated from the study area like the rays of a sun. She looked past them to the door to the librarian's office.

'You can see it all from up here.' The sound echoed around the chalky-looking plasterwork of the domed ceiling. 'This would have been a great place to keep watch from.'

Nedly looked at her doubtfully. 'I don't know – you'd have to keep pretty quiet.'

'I can be quiet.' Lil's voice bowled around the dome like a pinball and Nedly grinned at her. She took the pencil out of her mouth but all that chewing had made it too small to write with so she chucked it into her rucksack with the other stubs and then pulled out a spare and her notebook and laid them on one of the tilted reading desks. A dog-eared index card fell onto the floor. Nedly stared at it, pointed the tip of his glowing finger, and the card rose into the air.

'You dropped this,' he said.

Lil glanced up. She tried to suppress a fleeting look of panic and made a grab for the card with a muttered 'Thanks' but Nedly swiped it away for a closer look.

He stepped out of her reach as he twirled it around and floated the card in front of his eyes. 'This isn't the one for black tourmaline. It says here, "Selznick, Roland".'

Lil lurched forward, snatched it out of the air and stuffed it into her pocket.

Nedly's eyes widened. 'You're not supposed to keep hold of those – what if someone else needs it?'

Lil looked pointedly round at the empty library.

'I mean in the future.' Nedly held her gaze.

'I'm only borrowing it. I just need to use it a lot and I thought it would be easier if I kept hold of it, temporarily.'

'So Logan knows you have it?'

Lil rolled her eyes at him with a puff. She had worked out a cover story weeks ago for just this kind of eventuality.

'The fact is I'm thinking of writing a book about him, so I've been reading the reports he made before he was published under the pseudonym McNair, along with all the other Klaxon reporters. Once I get familiar with his style I bet I'll be able to identify which stories were his and then I can use them to tell the whole tale, about the Klaxon and McNair and him being rubbed out – all of it.'

Nedly thought about this for a moment. 'Won't that be dangerous, for the other Klaxon reporters, if you expose them?'

'I won't publish it. Not yet. Not until it's safe, but I will write it.'

'Sounds plausible.' Nedly gave her a lopsided smile and the tips of Lil's ears reddened. He pointed at a pencil and rolled it around a bit. 'I thought you were going to say it was because you wondered if maybe he was your real dad.'

The pencil rolled off the desk and pinged on

the floor with a crack that echoed around the mezzanine. Lil held her breath and then said, 'I suppose there's that too.' She looked sideways at him. 'He's probably not. It's just that my dad isn't around, for whatever reason, and neither is Selznick, because he's dead, so that's a pretty good reason not to be around, maybe the best reason of all.' She raised her eyebrows hopefully. 'Anyway, that's my theory. I'm going to follow it, see where it leads.'

'Why don't you just ask your mum?'

'I don't know; why doesn't she just tell me? Why do I have to ask? Anyway, I thought maybe she was in love with him.' Lil shrugged awkwardly. 'If she really liked him, I suppose she's pretty sad about it all.'

'Maybe, but that doesn't mean that she doesn't want to talk about him.'

'I like reading about him in any case. I just wanted to do that for now and if it's not him, then I don't want to know. Not yet.' She outstared Nedly until he shrugged and then said, 'Come on, we've got work to do.'

Lil referred to the other index card. There were three entries under black tourmaline: *qualities; uses in crystal healing; uses in folklore and mythology.* She ran her finger along the spines of the books until she found the number that corresponded to the first reference: *The Handbook of Gemstone Identification* by Professor Percival Somerset and flicked to the relevant page. There was a picture of a shiny black crystal, ridged slightly, like a boiled sweet, something liquorice-flavoured.

Nedly nodded confirmation. 'That's the stuff.'

Lil scanned through the paragraph below:

Black tourmaline is rarely used as a decorative gem but has an ability to generate electric charge under mechanical stress or change in shape when voltage is applied. It is naturally polarised and as a result can contain large electric fields.

'Electricity! So maybe they're not selling it at all – maybe they're using it themselves for something.'

Nedly's eyes widened. 'As some kind of fuel!'

'I'm pretty sure that the backpacks they use are battery-powered. Maybe they need the tourmaline for charging them up?' Lil tore a strip of wood from the end of her pencil and chewed on it thoughtfully. 'We should run it by Monbatsu; he's an egghead. He might understand all this science.'

Nedly frowned. 'But why do they need so much of it all of a sudden?'

The next reference was for *The Secret Power of Crystals and How to Use Them* by Janessa Ngata.

Lil found the book and flicked to the right page. She propped her head on her hand and read aloud.

'*Black tourmaline is the most commonly recommended crystal for protection, a powerful absorber of negative electromagnetic energy. It will create a boundary between the wearer and any unsavoury manifestation.*'

The echoes of her words chased each other

around the dome. Nedly looked troubled. 'A manifestation . . . like a ghost?'

Lil screwed up her face. 'I'm not sure. Ghostcatcher are all scientists . . . would they believe in the healing power of crystals?'

'Maybe they're mass-producing bracelets or something out of the tourmaline? People could wear them to protect them from things like –' his face fell – 'me?'

'I don't know,' Lil sighed wearily. 'This is all beginning to sound a bit far-fetched.'

There was one last reference and the book was *Sorting Through Shadows: Thirty Years' Experiences as a Ghost Hunter* by Milkwood James. Lil gave Nedly a look that said, *This will be the one,* and stuck her pencil in her hair. The section they needed was only a couple of bays away. Lil scanned the shelf, reading the numbers aloud. Then she backtracked. 'It should be right here.' She checked the shelves three times and then the ones above and below to be certain. The books were loose, as though one of them was missing. 'Nedly, it's been stolen!'

'Or maybe someone borrowed it?' he suggested.

'Maybe.' Lil narrowed her eyes. 'But who?'

She knocked firmly on the door to the librarian's office. Logan opened it just enough to stick out her head, framed as ever with short steel-grey hair and green-rimmed glasses. Several feet below, Milton, the library cat stuck his sleek head out too, took one look at Nedly and hissed. Logan gave Lil a look that said, *You're early* and then raised her eyebrows and Lil handed her the index card – tapping the entry for the missing book and shrugging.

Logan sighed. She hesitated for a moment and then stepped out of the office and closed the door and went over to her desk. She opened a drawer and pulled out a thin wooden tray packed with faded blue cards, selected one from the middle and drew a large leather-bound tome out from a shelf under the counter and flicked through it. The book was filled with lines and lines of pencil writing with dates, titles and names. Logan's eyes scanned back and forth across the page and then stopped. She turned the book to face Lil and pointed.

Sorting Through Shadows had been checked out fifteen years earlier and never been returned. Lil followed the entry along to the borrower column and read the name that was written there.

It was Irving Starkey.

Chapter 7

The Peligan City
Paranormal Society

Irving Starkey was Peligan City's own amateur ghost hunter, even back when no one else believed in ghosts. Recently Starkey had passed a stolen file to the *Klaxon* so they could break the 'Haunted' story: the scoop that got everyone wound up about the Final Ghost in the first place. Nedly had felt sorry for him and Abe had thought he was a crank, but none of them could have predicted just how much trouble he would cause – until it was too late.

Abe, Lil and Margaret left the Zodiac behind the old derelict lido in Peligan City, and Nedly led them between the rows of lock-ups to the last building standing at the end of the road, an olde-worlde inn known as the Masonic Rooms.

Abe swung the door open and Lil stoppered it with her foot, silhouetting the trio against the grey morning light. They stood there for a moment taking in the almost empty bar, the carpet and wallpaper both heavily patterned but in opposing styles, and the padded seating upholstered in red velour and edged with brass tacks. There was a stuffiness to the air and an old malty smell laced with the tang of vinegar.

The barman placed his palms wide on the highly polished wood counter and said, 'What can I get you?'

Abe propped up the bar and ordered two lemonades and a bag of crisps while Lil and Nedly browsed the jukebox.

When the drinks arrived, Abe paid up, took a sip and then said casually, 'We're here for the –' he dropped his voice – 'Paranormal Society.'

The barman paused in his polishing and gave them a relieved grin. 'You've come to the right place.'

'Happen to know if Irving Starkey still runs that show? We were hoping to bump into him.'

The barman's smile dipped and he eyed Abe suspiciously. 'I hope you're not here to make trouble; Irving's all right.'

Abe gave the barman a look like he wouldn't know how to make trouble if he tried and flapped an expired warrant card at him like a big leather moth. 'We just want to ask him a few questions.'

The barman looked sideways at where Lil was sitting. 'You and that kid?'

'I meant we, the police in general, want his help with our enquiries.'

'Well, he shouldn't be long.' The barman sighed. 'He's always here.'

The lights in the room dimmed a notch and the jukebox came on with a medley of banjo renditions of popular tunes.

Lil raised her eyebrows at Nedly. Margaret whined.

'I didn't mean to choose that one,' he protested.

'Can you make it stop?' Lil muttered.

The record scratched to the next song. 'Hey!' the barman warned. 'Don't mess around with that.'

Lil held her hands up in surrender, gave Nedly a dark look and then they trailed over to join Abe at the small table.

'Thanks,' said Lil, tearing open the bag of crisps and laying it flat for everyone to help themselves. Nedly nudged one out of the pack and across the table and over the side, where it dropped into Margaret's zone. Abe picked up yesterday's edition of the *Herald* from the next table and opened it to give them cover.

Lil elbowed Abe sharply in the side but it was too late. Nedly had already seen the headline. The inside story was 'Final Ghost Strikes at the Tin Pins Bowling Alley'.

He hung his head. 'Now I can never go back there. I'm running out of places to hang out,' he said. There was desperation in his voice but he attempted to cover it with a grim smile.

Lil returned it, but he was right.

She murmured her way through the first paragraph: '*Bowler complains of haunted shoes – missed a strike and lost game when the Final Ghost turned up.*' She dismissed it with a scowl. 'No one is going to believe that.'

'I did scare someone at the bowling alley yesterday,' Nedly admitted. 'I didn't mean to. I was just watching the game and someone came and sat on me. But I spooked them, not the shoes.'

'They probably just wanted to get a refund on the hire charge.'

'Hey!' Abe hissed. 'Here he is.' He stretched the paper out so it covered their faces and then lowered it slightly so he could peer over it. Lil tugged on the bottom edge of it so that she

could see over too, exposing Abe's whole face and shoulders.

Irving Starkey stood frozen in the doorway staring at Abe. His green waterproof poncho hung from his shoulders, his shining bald head and orange aviator glasses spotted with rain.

'He's going to run!' Lil whispered.

But Starkey didn't run. He ran a hand over his neat goatee beard and walked slowly to the bar. His voice was crackly as he said, 'Ginger beer please, Tom.'

Abe folded the newspaper and then dropped it onto the seat beside him. The bartender put a tall glass of ginger beer on the counter and an empty plate, and then Irving turned and walked ceremoniously over to where Abe and Lil were sitting.

He pulled up a stool and took his rucksack from his shoulders, reached inside and pulled out a large packet of custard creams and shook them out onto the plate.

He looked at Lil and Abe and then let his gaze linger at the empty pew beside them.

Margaret got to her feet and gave his hand the once-over with her wet nose.

'Hello, strange little dog.' He patted her tentatively on the head. 'I was expecting you.' He looked quickly up at Abe and Lil. 'I mean . . . I was expecting all of you.' His eyes searched the room again.

Lil snorted.

Abe looked around. 'I would have thought with all the interest in the Final Ghost these meetings would be packed.'

Starkey looked sadly into his ginger beer. 'People don't want to investigate ghosts; they just want rid of them.'

'Whose fault is that?' Lil muttered. She gave Starkey the Squint. 'Why were you expecting us?'

Starkey looked surprised. 'Because of my note.'

'What note?' It was Lil's turn to look surprised.

They sat looking at each other until Abe broke the tension with a crunch of biscuit.

Lil resharpened the Squint. '*Sorting Through*

108

Shadows ring any bells?' Starkey's bemused expression told her that it didn't. 'It's a book you borrowed from the library.'

'Very possibly you are correct,' he admitted. 'But the library has been closed for more than a decade now.'

'I'm aware of that,' Lil snipped back. 'Did you think that meant you could just keep the things you borrowed from it?'

Starkey's cheeks coloured. 'I couldn't return it after the library closed; how could I?'

'You could have posted it through the door.'

'Who would have collected it – the building is all boarded up?'

Abe interrupted. 'I think we're getting side-tracked –'

Starkey continued in earnest: 'How did you even know I'd borrowed it?'

Lil searched the glass rings on the table looking for some way out. 'That's not the point, as in, it's part of an ongoing investigation, as in, I'm not at liberty to say.' She folded her arms.

Abe cut in again, pointing with a second custard cream for emphasis. 'We need some information that was in that book. Information about the uses of a mineral called black tourmaline.'

Starkey's eyes lit up. 'Of course! The same black tourmaline that is being delivered to the secret Ghostcatcher facility out at Rorschach Asylum and has been authorised and funded by Acting Mayor Gordian.'

Abe choked on his biscuit. 'You know about that?'

Nedly's eyes widened. 'You're "A friend"!'

Lil gave him a look that suggested otherwise and then joined the dots. 'You sent the anonymous note! Why didn't you just say it was you?'

'I didn't think you would trust me.' He looked around again. 'I – I realise now that I made a grave error of judgement when I gave that newsletter the Fright File story, and now I fear that something uniquely wonderful would be lost if I don't try and stop them.'

'Stop who?'

'Ghostcatcher.'

The banjo music wobbled and skipped and Irving pricked his ears up and his eyes grew bright.

'*You* are a ghost catcher,' Lil reminded him. 'I thought you were all for catching ghosts?'

'I'm a ghost hunter; there's a difference. Before the Fright File I only wanted to know if ghosts were real, to find that elusive evidence, proof of the afterlife. I want to help you,' he added.

'We don't need your help.' Lil scowled. 'Just give us the book back.'

'It's not your book either.' Irving frowned. 'It belongs to the library.'

Abe cleared his throat. 'We just need to know about that mineral. If you could fill us in, it would save some time.'

Starkey smiled. 'Black tourmaline is a powerful defensive gem, historically used by paranormal investigators to ward off negative energy from spirits, or, I suppose, on a greater scale, to provide a shield from the effects of hauntings.'

Lil flicked through her writing pad to find the notes she had made in the library and began adding Starkey's information.

'Under certain circumstances it is capable of both generating and containing electricity. You see, the tourmaline draws energy from the spirit itself and uses it against them. I believe it's the basis for the EMF readers that Ghostcatcher uses and also their Projected Entrapment Matrix.' When he saw the expression on Lil and Abe's faces Starkey explained: 'The green laser net.'

'They must burn through a lot of it if they have shipments coming in every other night,' said Lil. 'They haven't actually successfully captured a ghost in weeks.'

Abe tried to kick Lil under the table but caught Starkey instead. The ghost hunter winced and tears pooled in his eyes. When he recovered he said, 'Indeed, and it's highly toxic after use so disposal would be an expensive business – not something to be undertaken lightly. I think that it's imperative to discover what they are using it for now, and I was hoping you could help me find out.'

Abe rubbed his chin with his rubber hand. 'Who's to say we would be interested in all this anyway?'

Starkey looked baffled. 'You certainly sound interested.'

Lil's ear tips burned. She cast a quick glance at Nedly and then Starkey's lively eyes met hers in earnest.

'You are, though, aren't you?' He let his gaze drift around the room again and then he removed his orange-tinted spectacles. 'I don't think these work after all,' he said sadly and took them off, leaving behind symmetrical red marks on his nose where they had rested. 'Is he here?' Lil looked at Abe. 'No, the ghost,' Starkey insisted. 'Is he here now?'

Lil froze for a millisecond and then started to her feet.

'Please,' he said. 'I mean no harm. I'm afraid

it turns out that whatever it is people have that allows them to feel the presence of spirits, I just don't have it. Even though it is all I've ever wanted.' He gave a melancholy laugh. 'I suppose life is like that sometimes.

'The accounts I received from my contact, Craig Weasel, the so-called Fright File and my dealings with Ghostcatcher led me to believe that the Haunting of Peligan City was perpetrated by a most malevolent spirit or spirits. A terrible threat to the safety of the citizens. But since then I have been tracking the exploits of the one they call the Final Ghost – and I don't mean by these attention-grabbing ghost stories –' he pointed disdainfully at the *Herald* – 'but the facts – and a very different picture has emerged. I no longer believe that the Final Ghost is terrorising the city. In fact, my research suggests a different story entirely.'

Lil gave Nedly an imperceptible shake of the head and thinned out her lips. 'It's too late for that now,' she said. 'Even if there was a Final

Ghost, you've already turned everyone against him.'

Starkey slumped his shoulders miserably. 'If I could go back . . .'

'Well, you can't.' Lil scowled at him. 'And you're one hundred and ten per cent wrong again: there is no last ghost; Ghostcatcher are just draining the city purse, getting everyone in a panic. Gordian might be genuine and clean but the Final Ghost still is a convenient smokescreen to distract people from worrying about all the things in Peligan City that need to be put right. Anyone can see that.' She crossed her arms.

Starkey looked at her. 'I've been following your cases, observing how you –'

'Spying on us?'

'Not spying . . . I just needed to know, if it was true.'

Abe poured the last of the crisp crumbs into his mouth and put the bag down with a crackle. 'I told you the last time –'

'I know, detective, you don't believe in ghosts.'

The lights on the jukebox dimmed and the banjo twanking slowed down, becoming slightly off-key. He listened for a moment and then added, 'But I do.'

'Thanks for the tip-off.' Abe nodded sagely. 'But you've got the wrong gang. I thought there might be a link to organised crime with that business down at the docks but it looks as if it's just more hooey so it's not really our bag.' He looked a bit shamefaced. 'No hard feelings.'

'None.' Irving smiled bravely. 'But if I can help, if there's anything . . .' He pressed a handwritten business card into Lil's hand. 'I'm at your disposal.'

Lil flipped it back onto the table saying, 'Whatever,' and followed Abe to the door. She held it open for a moment, but Nedly lingered, saying, 'I'll catch you up.'

Irving Starkey took a last sip of ginger beer and surveyed the pile of biscuits on the plate. He picked one up, took a small bite and chewed it slowly. He closed his eyes, gulped it away, sighed deeply and said to the barman, 'I think

I'll head off myself. I don't expect anyone else will come today.'

He got to his feet and began clearing the table. When he saw the plate of biscuits he frowned. His hand trembled as he pulled it closer. Starkey caught his breath, swivelled the plate round, and tears sprang to his eyes. The custard creams had been rearranged into an odd formation: one short line and two longer ones with a sideways biscuit in the middle. They spelled a single word: 'HI'.

Beaming, Starkey turned to the barman and lifted the plate. 'Look!' All the biscuits slid off and torpedoed the floor.

'Are you all right, Irving?'

Starkey put a hand to his chest to calm his fluttering heart and nodded eagerly. 'I'm better than all right. Hello, my friend. Hello at last!' he cried out, as the tears made a break from his eyes and trickled down his cheeks.

Chapter 8

The Lick and Spittle
Boxing Club

The next morning at the Nite Jar, Lil had just rolled up her sleeves to start washing the pots when there was a phone call for her.

She took the receiver cautiously and frowned down the line before saying, 'Hello?'

'Lil Potkin?'

'Who is this?'

The voice on the other end spoke fast and low. 'It's me, Irving Starkey. Your friend is in great danger. You must warn him. Last night I . . .'

A no-nonsense voice cut in. 'I thought you were calling a solicitor?

Lil heard Starkey say, 'Wrong number,' and the phone went dead.

'Hello? Hello?' Lil called into the receiver. Her heart was racing. Quickly she dialled another number. After twelve rings Abe picked up, and before he had a chance to speak Lil said, 'Is Nedly with you?'

Abe paused. 'What? No, I – I don't think so. Wait.' Lil heard him say something to Margaret then he returned to the line. 'I don't think so.'

Lil's pulse thumped warningly in her ears. 'I think we better find him.'

She pushed her rising panic into something she could use, left her apron on the sideboard and ten minutes later she and Abe were pounding the rain-slick streets with Margaret jogging behind them, her eyes and nose on the job as she weaved expertly between the puddles.

'It's just round the corner,' said Lil as they

took a shortcut through a narrow alley and came out at an old disused car park. When Abe stepped into the dull light of day his face darkened.

Crouched under a curved brick railway bridge was a single-storey building with a flat roof. A sign painted on the front in flaking pink letters read 'Carl's Gym'. A yellow light smouldered behind a row of high narrow windows. It looked as sturdy as a bomb shelter.

Abe eyed it all grimly. 'You're sure this is the place?'

'It's one of Nedly's regular haunts. He likes to come down here to watch the fights, pick up some tips.'

The atmosphere felt heavy, like a storm was brewing. The wind splashed rain in their faces.

Abe looked over his shoulder. 'So we don't know for sure if he's here?'

'He won't go back to the bowling alley on account of the spooky-shoes story. He's not at our home or at yours, I've already checked the library and he's not at the Nite Jar. It's the only place left.' Lil stepped forward. Abe didn't move; his body swayed but it was like his feet had grown roots. She looked up at him. 'If he's not here, I don't know where he is.'

Abe took a couple of deep breaths through his nostrils and let the last one out with a gruff snort. 'All right,' he said finally. 'Let's get this over with.'

He walked quickly to the side of the gym, flattened himself against the concrete wall and glanced round the corner at the door.

Lil stood beside him. 'Shall we knock?'

Abe gave the door a grim appraisal. 'I'm just figuring out how to play it.'

Margaret let out a sharp bark.

'Shhh!' hissed Abe. 'We're trying to keep a low profile here.'

'Could've fooled me.' A bass voice cut through the air, smooth with a side order of menace.

The colour drained from Abe's face. 'Sweets Mayhem! Fancy meeting you here.' His tone was light but the laugh that followed had a desperate sound to it.

Sweets Mayhem cast a shadow that eclipsed the grey morning light. Lil squinted up at him. The boxer's head was mostly covered by the hood of his sweatsuit and she could only make out a wide jaw, and puffed eyelids. She tried to sound casual. 'We're just looking for somewhere to train, but we thought we should check it out first, before we bothered anyone.'

Sweets' humourless eyes stared back at her. 'It's no bother.' His neck was wrapped in cords of muscle that flexed as he tilted his head at her. 'I'll walk you in.'

He herded them round the corner, his hands scrunching their collars tightly round their necks and then eased them towards a heavy metal door studded with rivets. Abe knocked lightly on it. No answer. He took a step back but the boxer was right behind him and Abe trod on his toes. Sweets didn't flinch, he just pushed Abe back up to the door until his belly was against it and this time he knocked for him. A big pounding fist.

Lil kept trying to catch Abe's eye. She could see the muscles working his jaw as he chewed on the situation. The slot in the door opened and a pair of heavily wrinkled eyes peered out. Abe dropped his chin so the rim of his hat shadowed his face.

Sweets said, 'Found these two sneaking around outside.'

The eyes narrowed at Abe. 'Don't I know you from somewhere?'

'I have one of those faces.'

The eyes swelled for a second, then said, 'No dogs.' There was a sound of metal bolts being scraped across and then finally the door opened. It was at least three inches thick.

'Stay,' Abe told Margaret.

As they were shoved inside Lil glanced over her shoulder to see the small figure of Margaret sitting alone in the rain and then the heavy door swung shut and they were trapped.

'What's going on?' Lil hissed.

'Leave the talking to me.' Abe's face was set now, Easter Island style. 'Just find the kid and get out. Any chance you get.'

'What?' Lil gasped and then they were being hustled down a narrow corridor past photos of famous fights, some publicity shots of Sweets, fists raised in front of his pinched head, alongside signed pictures of more famous visiting boxers and a couple of group photos labelled 'Lick and Spittle Boxing Club'. That name rang a bell; Lil had heard it somewhere before. She looked back at Abe, and a sinking feeling grew in her belly. She remembered the story now – back when Abe had been on the Squad, he had brought down a large-scale protection racket based out of the Lick and Spittle Boxing Club. But that was years ago. Surely no one would remember it.

As they entered the gym Lil scanned the room quickly: there were bodies, lots of them, in vests and shorts and sweatsuits. No Nedly, but there was a door on the other side of the boxing ring. She caught Abe's eye and pointed to it.

He gave her a discreet nod and then a voice cut through the buzz of the room, dulling it to silence.

'Can I believe my eyes?' A short man with a fuzz of white hair and a satin shirt he was making his way towards them at a leisurely pace. The boxers moved aside as he passed through and then surged behind him like a wave of muscle.

'Detective Mandrel!' He looked like he couldn't believe his luck. His shirt was unbuttoned to mid-chest where six or seven gold chains lay. 'All that time I spent in the Needle, hoping I'd run in to you again one day and you walk right onto my turf – easy as pie.'

'Nicky Vega. So this is your joint now?' Abe met his gaze. 'What happened to Quick Fingal?'

'He wasn't quick enough,' Vega snarled and then laughed. 'And it's legit.' The surrounding boxers drew closer in round them.

'I'll bet,' said Abe, his jaw clenched in a steely way. Lil pressed her elbow into his. Abe unclenched his jaw. 'I'm not looking for faces.'

'What *are* you looking for?'

Abe rubbed his chin with his rubber hand and gave Lil a look, flicking his gaze away, which said, *Go and find Nedly.* He tried to break a smile at Vega. 'I'm looking for somewhere . . . to work out.' The room went silent and Abe hoisted his belt up over his belly and craned his neck out of his collar. 'And this place looked . . . pretty good.' He nodded approvingly at the bare concrete floor, the sweating walls, the punchbags shiny with knuckle grease, and the dirty towels.

Vega poked a finger at Abe's damp shirt. 'Last time you crossed my threshold it was with a squad of cops and a battering ram. Who's this, your coach?' He nodded at Lil and jabbed Sweets in the belly. Sweets didn't blink but snorted out a laugh on cue.

'I'm off duty; like I said, I just came in to check out the facilities.' Abe pointed towards the ring, stepping in front of Lil who stepped backwards at the same time and slipped out of the crowd.

'This isn't a free floor show, Mandrel. If you want to see a fight, you're going to have to pay for it just like everyone else.'

'I'm not here for a fight,' he explained to the three burly boxers who had stepped towards him menacingly.

Lil backed away from the circle that was gathering, and darted quickly past the climbing bars strung with plump leather boxing gloves and ducked into an empty locker room. 'Nedly!' she called out. 'Nedly, where are you?'

'I'm here,' came a voice from behind a door.

Lil opened it. It was an equipment cupboard. The shelves were stacked with rolls of bandages, spare gloves and skipping ropes. A couple of medicine balls were on the floor.

'Are you hiding?'

'I was just working on some moves,' Nedly said, delivering a couple of jabs to the air.

'Pretty good.'

He left the cupboard and came to sit on the wooden bench in the centre of the room. Lil slid onto it beside him.

'It smells like socks in here,' she said.

'I can't smell anything.'

'You're lucky.'

Nedly bent forward and wrapped his arms round his knees. 'So . . . ?'

Lil paused. 'So, we didn't know where you were, and –' She glanced nervously over her shoulder. 'We can't really stick around. I didn't make the connection but Abe's got history here. He's in the middle of accounting for it now, so we should split soon as.' She got to her feet and headed for the door.

Nedly hesitated. 'Thanks for checking in on me but I'm fine.' He didn't look fine. 'You can go.'

Lil gave him a disapproving frown and decided to come clean. 'We just got a call, from Starkey. He said you're in danger.'

'So, now you trust Starkey?'

'No, but . . . he sounded serious. We've got to stick together. You have to keep your head down now.'

'My head is down. I was in the cupboard, remember? I'm not bothering anyone.'

'What if someone gets the creeps and reports you? We have to keep moving.'

Nedly gave her a dark look. 'Stop saying "we"; it's just me that's in danger.'

Lil fixed him with a Squint. 'I think we're all in danger now.' She pushed open the door to the locker room and held it open. They looked out into the gym.

Abe was being muscled into the ring by Sweets Mayhem, who took hold of his mac and shook it off him, taking the rubber hand with it.

'Hey,' Abe cried. 'That's expensive.' Sweets gave him a disbelieving snort. 'The hand, I mean. I had to have it made.' Abe was holding his multi-function pincer up in protest. 'You see? My boxing days are over.'

'I thought you were here looking for somewhere to train?'

'He is.' Lil ran forward, shouting out over the jeers. 'For me.' She bent under the ropes, strode into the ring and squared up to the boxer's belly, holding her chin up.

'Get out of the ring, Wing Nut. We've got a score to settle,' Vega shouted to her from the sidelines.

Lil put her hands on her hips. 'We've got nothing to prove to you. We just came in to check the place out, we've checked it and now we're going.' She took hold of Abe's sleeve. Sweets smirked at her and then with one huge arm picked her up by the scruff of her rain mac and lifted her over the ropes, dropping her unceremoniously on the other side.

He raised his bulbous glove at her and said. 'It's an insult to the boss that Mandrel came back here and he knows it. He owes him an apology.'

'I'm sorry,' said Abe through gritted teeth.

Sweets pulled Abe's new hat down round his ears and then flattened the crown until it looked more like a boater. 'Better put this on nice and tight – don't want it falling off.'

The owner of the craggy eyes turned out to be a wiry old man in a cloth cap and caretaker dungarees. He clanked the bell ringside and everyone drew in to watch. Abe appealed to him. 'Where's your sense of fair play? I'm out of shape and more than twice his age.'

Vega clapped his hands together as though he was about to sit down to a banquet.

Sweets Mayhem started circling round and then he sprang up and down on his toes a couple of times, circled back and put up his fists.

'Come on, old man, show me what you've got.'

Abe nodded towards Lil. 'At least let the kid go; she doesn't need to see this.'

'She's free to go any time she pleases.'

'I'm staying.' Lil folded her arms but her eyes darted around until they found Nedly's and they exchanged nervous glances.

Abe shrugged as whatever fight was there left him. 'All right, let me have it.'

Sweets poked Abe in the shoulder. 'You first.'

Abe half-heartedly hit Sweets in his belly, Sweets pushed Abe's chin back up with one hand and drove a piledriver in with the other.

Abe reeled, shaking his head to clear it. He felt his jaw gingerly and then swung wide with his left. Sweets bobbed easily to avoid it. He was coming up again with a jab while Abe's fist was still in motion. Sweets delivered the jab to Abe's right side and then his second fist followed up on the left straight after.

Abe doubled over, coughing. 'I give up,' he wheezed.

'Not yet you don't.'

Abe held his right elbow up to shield himself and hefted with his left, trying to get some kind of rhythm together.

Sweets shook his head like it was embarrassing to watch.

'You shouldn't have come!' cried Nedly. 'He's going to get minced.'

'Abe!' Lil yelled, darting towards the ropes, but a boxer standing nearby put a hand that felt more like an anvil on her shoulder and left it there. Lil tried to shrink out from under it but he had her pinned. 'Help him!' Lil said.

'Ain't no one can help him now,' the boxer

replied matter-of-factly, adding a couple of pounds to the anvil.

Nedly gave Lil a firm nod and then pushed up the sleeves of his thin grey sweater and stepped into the ring behind Abe.

Abe took another swipe. Sweets stepped aside to avoid it. He threw a look at Vega.

Vega shrugged back. 'Get it over with.'

Abe ducked the next punch and then got one in the belly. He crumpled against the ropes.

'Come on, is that the best you've got? You're embarrassing your little girl.'

Abe glanced sideways and caught Lil out of the corner of his eye. She didn't look embarrassed. She looked determined. 'Show him what you're made of!' she yelled. Abe started to shake his head in defeat, but the look in Lil's eye was pure steel. Abe gulped then nodded.

As Sweets drew back a fist, a shadow seemed to move across the ring, and he whipped his head round to catch it. At the same time Abe pulled back his left, and loosed it as Nedly swept in behind, adding his glowing hand to

Abe's swing. The punch drove Sweets off his enormous feet, and he pirouetted on the diagonal as he went down. By the time he hit the deck he was out cold.

The crowd fell silent in shock. The lights flickered on and off, the punching bags began swaying on their own and the air chilled by several degrees as a wave of unfathomable dread spread through the room. The caretaker stood dumbfounded for a moment and then rang the bell. He hopped through the ropes to administer some slaps and a squirt of water to revive Sweets Mayhem. Nedly stood anxiously by until the boxer opened his eyes.

Abe shivered, stretching out the fingers of his trembling left hand to check he hadn't broken them. He wiped the sweat out of his eyebrows with the back of his shirt sleeve, took his hat off, pushed the crown out and redented it and then replaced it on his head. As he walked from the ring Lil handed him his coat and rubber hand. He re-attached it and then he dusted off his palms.

With a nod to Vega and the gang they walked through the silent gym. The wrinkly-eyed caretaker opened the door for them. As they passed he stopped Lil and said, 'You really interested in training?'

Lil shrugged. 'Maybe one day.'

'Tell you what. If you want to fight, look me up. If you can punch like your old man, then you might have a future here.'

Abe was still shaking when they emerged into the cold, wet air of the empty car park. The pale sun had drained out of the sky and dark clouds had moved in.

Margaret looked relieved to see them in one piece.

'Sorry I didn't listen to the warning, little pal,' Abe told her.

He trained his eyes on an empty spot by Lil. 'And thanks for the help with the punch, kid. You've given me a whole new kind of history there.' He straightened his collar and tie and shrugged his mac so it was a little squarer on his shoulders. 'Now, how about we get a hot

135

chocolate? On me. I could do with something.'
He shivered.

Lil looked up at the sky; it was thick with
the incoming storm. 'Maybe we should get off
the streets, at least until we can figure out what
Starkey meant. What do you think, Nedly?'

Nedly opened his mouth to reply and then
Margaret started barking as bright magnesium
headlights scorched over the weedy concrete
like white-hot laser beams. A silver van careered
round the corner.

'Nedly . . .' Lil's eyes were wide. 'RUN!'

Nedly turned so fast that he stumbled. Lil
lurched forward to help him up but her hand
just grabbed thin air. As Nedly scrambled to
his feet Lil whipped round to face the lights.
Nedly hurdled the low wall of the car park and
Lil ran into the path of the van, forcing it to
skid on the wet ground as it tried to avoid her.
Abe caught up, yanking Lil back by her mac
and then turning shoulder-on to block the
oncoming vehicle.

It skidded to a halt only feet away from them.

Virgil leapt from the van, almost speechless with fury and slammed the door. She marched over to Abe. 'What do you think you're doing!' Then she did a double take. 'You again!'

Abe shrugged. He tried to look casual but his face was pale and clammy-looking.

Lil spoke up. 'There's something going on – at the boxing club.' She pointed to it. 'The punch bags are moving on their own and it's freezing and really creepy in there.' Marek hurtled out of the cab, yanked open the sliding door and Yossarian climbed out of the back. He handed the other two their helmets and they swiftly attached harnesses.

Virgil kept a warning eye on Lil and Abe, up until her helmet went on. As she passed them she paused and they saw their own faces reflected in the orange visor, smaller and further away than they really were.

Marek followed her but Yossarian hung back a little and gave Lil a shrug that suggested, *Sorry about the other two*. He hesitated as if he was going to add something else, but changed his mind, put on his helmet too and jogged after them.

As soon as they were clear Lil checked that Nedly was out of sight and then whispered 'That was too close.'

'Much too close.' Abe glared at her and shook his head despairingly.

There were raised voices at the door to the boxing club; the scientists were trying to talk their way in without much luck.

Lil tried to gulp away the feeling of dread that was tightening around her windpipe like a vice. 'They're going to get him, you know, if we're not careful.'

She searched Abe for an answer. He raised his hands as though he had hold of something they could use and then let whatever it was fall. He sighed. 'We'll think of something.' But they both knew that it was going to be their toughest case yet.

Chapter 9

We Need to Talk about Roland Selznick

Lil sat on the arm of the saggy chair by the window in the front room. The rain appeared on the glass as clear, round dots that broke their shape and trickled downwards, the patterns changing every second. Dusk had come to Angel Lane and the alleyways opposite were murky with shadows.

'Are you OK?' Naomi switched on the light, illuminating the room and plunging the world outside into darkness. 'You've been staring out of that window for hours. Are you waiting for someone? I thought you were out with Quake tonight.'

'I didn't feel up to it.'

Naomi felt Lil's forehead. She stood next to her at the window. 'Anything you want to talk about?'

Lil shrugged.

'Come on,' said Naomi. 'Waldo's place could do with a spruce up. I'll give you a hand.'

Standing side by side in the utility room Lil and her mum tore the *Herald* into strips, obliterating any sign of the stories it held. As an employee of City Hall, Naomi was sent a compulsory copy of the paper every morning; they took the money for it out of her wages.

Waldo was sitting on the drainer in a shoebox with a few holes punched in the lid. Lil could hear him scratching inside, testing the integrity of the cardboard walls with his tiny pale claws.

Naomi turned on the tap full blast and squirted a bowl with washing-up liquid while Lil tipped the old bedding into the compost bin and squashed it down.

'This is getting pretty full,' she said at the exact same time her mum said: 'Lil, we need to talk about Roland Selznick.'

An awkward silence followed.

Lil broke it first. 'What did you say?'

'Oh, nothing,' Naomi said, thrashing the washing-up brush around in the soapy water for a moment. 'No, it's not nothing. It's just . . .' She braced her rubber-gloved hands against the edge of the sink. 'I was thinking, perhaps . . .' She took a deep breath. 'We need to talk about Roland Selznick.' Lil stared into the bin. Naomi picked up the brush again and began scrubbing and dunking the plastic floor of Waldo's cage. 'That reporter I used to know. Back when I –'

'The one who died.'

'He was killed, yes, that one.'

Lil kept her eyes on the contents of the bin.

'Was he my father?' she asked suddenly and then immediately felt sick.

Naomi stopped scrubbing. She dropped the brush and left it to sink beneath the water, while she turned to face Lil.

Lil cautiously returned the bin lid and looked across at her mother.

They stood staring at each other for what felt like hours. Naomi looked almost as afraid as Lil felt now that the question had been asked and must be answered.

'He was,' she said.

Lil's throat felt she had swallowed a bowling ball but she managed to whisper, 'Thought so.'

She picked up the old tea towel and Naomi reached into the sink and pulled out the floor of the cage and passed it to Lil, who began drying it.

When Lil felt she could talk normally again she said, 'What was he like then?'

Naomi leant back against the sink, peeled off her rubber gloves and hung them on the drainer.

'He was a great investigative reporter.'

'I mean as a person.'

Naomi searched the ceiling for the answer and then shrugged. 'He was funny and . . . I suppose you would say . . . confident? I don't think he cared what other people thought of him.'

'He must have cared what you thought,' Lil said.

Naomi laughed. 'Yes, I suppose he must have done.'

'Am I like him?'

Naomi puffed out a sigh. 'In some ways you are.' Her bespectacled eyes had an uncertain look about them. She tucked Lil's hair behind her ears. 'If I'm honest, I don't think I ever got beyond the surface, not before he . . . and now I'll never know. So to me, you're unquestionably just like you, and not like anyone else I know.'

'Abe says I'm like you.'

'It's the ears.'

'Not just the ears,' Lil corrected her. 'And coming from Abe it's a pretty big compliment.'

Naomi blushed and worked on shaking up the soapy water in Waldo's water bottle.

'I mean it,' said Lil, warming to the subject. 'It's probably the biggest compliment he could give anyone.' They elbowed each other playfully, both grinning and then Lil went back to her drying.

After a moment she said, 'Why didn't you tell me before?'

'About Roland? I didn't know how to tell you about him and still protect you from all that history with McNair and the *Chronicle* and the *Klaxon*; it was all so tangled up together.' She sighed and closed her eyes. 'And a part of me thought maybe you didn't need to know?'

The tea towel was damper than the floor of the cage now but Lil kept on rubbing it. 'I just wondered about it, that's all.' She took the water bottle and started polishing up the spout. 'Anyway, mystery solved.'

Naomi ruffled her hair. 'It wasn't much of a mystery.'

'It was to me,' Lil said.

Naomi's look sharpened as she took a sudden breath and then pulled Lil in for a vice-like bear hug, crushing the air out of her lungs. 'You're right. That was a stupid thing to say. If there's anything else you want to know, then just ask.'

She handed Lil a fresh tea towel. 'I've often wondered if maybe you thought it was Abe?'

'You would have told me if it was him.'

'If your dad had still been around, whoever he was, I would have told you. If there had been any chance of you getting to know him . . .' Naomi's fingers went to her lips. 'You didn't think he just didn't want to know you?'

Lil shrugged. 'I didn't know what to think. I didn't have much to go on, so . . .'

Naomi looked down. 'I'm sorry. I've mishandled it and now . . .'

Lil squeezed her hand. 'I just wanted to know, so I didn't have to spend all my time wondering about it, that's all.'

They carried Waldo's cage over to the

sideboard where it could be reassembled and then put down a layer of fresh newspaper and stuffed in a handful of the shredded *Herald*s for a good-sized nest. When it was done Lil took the lid off the shoebox and Waldo breathed the free air while she picked him up in her cupped hand and stroked him on the head. The hamster clutched at her thumb knuckle with his tiny paws and stared at his home. His nose twitched.

Waldo didn't like being held, so reluctantly Lil put him back in the cage. He looked suspiciously at the new layout and then did a couple of circuits to check on his belongings; he stoically accepted that his tangled nest of food and bedding were all gone. Instead there was a new, unfamiliar smelling clump of paper with no food in it. With an air of exasperation he pulled apart the scrunched nest that Lil had created, sombrely accepted the thin carrot stick she offered him and stashed it in his new pad and then he took his frustration out on the wheel.

'So,' said Naomi, as they watched Waldo scampering as fast as he could. 'How are you getting on at the *Klaxon*? Do you like working with Quake?'

'I like Quake but I'll be glad when Ghostcatcher throws in their cards so I can get on a proper news story.'

Naomi raised an intrigued eyebrow. 'You really think they'll give up before they catch it?'

Another sick feeling swelled in Lil's belly. 'Don't you?'

'I don't think they will stop any time soon.' Naomi shrugged matter-of-factly. 'There's too much at stake; as long as Sam Tangiers can keep the public's interest on the Final Ghost then no one is looking at City Hall and all the other things it should be doing to clean up the city. It's a fantastic distraction.'

Lil tried to keep the rush of panic out of her voice. 'But they can't just keep on, can they? Not for ever?'

Naomi gave her a sympathic arm-squeeze. 'I

know it's tough. Tracking a story like this is playing the long game and sometimes it can seem like it will never end but you have to hang in there. If you want to be around when something happens, you have to be around all the time. That's just how it works. Ask Abe – the P.I. business is mostly watching and waiting.'

The sick feeling welled up in Lil's throat, tightening it like a thick scarf.

'I –' she began. 'I can't explain it. I just don't think it's right to hunt someone down. If they haven't done anything wrong, then people should leave them alone.'

Naomi shrugged. 'But this isn't a person, Lil; it's a ghost – or at least it's the idea of a ghost.'

'You don't believe in any of it, do you?' Lil glanced sideways at her mother.

'No,' Naomi admitted. 'I don't buy the ghost story. I prefer to concentrate on things involving real people with real problems not make-believe spooks. That's the stuff of campfire stories and graveyards; it's not real life.'

Lil was glad that Nedly wasn't around to hear that, but then a small starburst of an idea lit up in her mind. If everyone thought like her mother did, then Ghostcatcher would have to be disbanded, and then maybe Nedly would be free again, maybe he would be safe. And if anyone was going to write a story about the non-existence of the Final Ghost, it would be Naomi Potkin.

'Maybe you're right,' Lil said cautiously. 'Maybe there is no Final Ghost.'

Naomi did a double take. 'I thought you were keeping an open mind?'

Lil chewed on the inside of her lip and hardened her face into a frown. 'I don't know what I believe any more.'

Outside, in the yard, Nedly looked in at them through the window, his eyes dark and sorrowful. Then he turned from the warm, inviting glow of number ten Angel Lane and walked away.

Chapter 10

The Golden Loop

From a distance the Golden Loop casinos looked like a heap of gold and jewels nestled amidst the mud of a murky seabed. On closer inspection it revealed the glitter was just paint and neon lighting that glowed up into the smog. Nevertheless the sparkling centre sucked all the life out of the rest of Peligan City, like a gigantic money-eating tick crouched at the heart of the metropolis.

Nedly hung back at the end of a darkened

alley and waited until his eyes had adjusted to the bright lights.

All the casinos had themes and the doormen dressed accordingly. At the Wheel of Fortune, close to where Nedly was standing, they were dressed as Roman centurions with gold lamé armour over faux satin minidresses, and shivered in the cold night air. The doormen were officially there to welcome patrons out of the rain and into the majesty of the casino floors, but they were built like security guards, with wide shoulders and fists like mallets. They were paid to throw people out when their money was gone, and to keep them away from the management when the house took it all, which it always did, in the end.

Above the door a six-metre-high roulette wheel turned slowly, its many bulbs flashing on and off. In front was a fountain lit so it looked like it was flowing with molten gold, but as Nedly passed it he saw that the water was brownish-green and had churned itself into scum.

At the entrance a purple carpet led up over

some shallow steps and between two pillars. Nedly stepped through the ornate plaster mouldings and into the huge room beyond. It was packed from wall to wall with a labyrinth of slot machines.

Every one was occupied by a person feeding in a coin at a time, but these machines were always hungry, no matter how much they ate.

Nedly moved quickly, skirting along the wall, head down, shoulders in, trying not to give anyone the creeps. The music was fast-paced and upbeat, and the faces of the people at the machines were haunted more by the idea of luck than by Nedly. A couple shivered as he passed but nothing more. He looked up to the roulette tables where the high rollers were gathered in evening suits and sequinned dresses.

The house always wins? *Well, not tonight*, he thought. He saw a woman with long dark hair pulled back tightly in a low bun and dark shadows under her eyes. Her navy blue quilted jacket was torn at the elbow and her black tights had a hole in them.

Nedly watched her put coin after coin into the machine, yank down the metal arm and watch the three wheels spin, hoping for a line-up of identical symbols in a row. As the pile in her left hand grew smaller the effort she put into pulling the lever grew greater.

So people thought the Final Ghost was a menace? Nedly knew that there were things he could do to help and prove himself, that there were ways he could try to turn things round. He took a breath, steeled himself and then quickly crept up to the back of the slot machine, and sank inside it. The mechanics of the device were lit up by the flashing buttons on the player's side, the three wheels spinning and clattering round like beads in a jar as they lined up one pineapple, two pineapples – and a watermelon. Nedly saw the player's face fall and her right hand go back to her left for another coin, but it was empty. It was now or never. Nedly gritted his teeth and pointed as hard as he could, until energy struck and lit his finger like a match head.

The watermelon began to very slowly click backwards. The player was patting down her pockets when a cold breath whispered across her skin and she looked up. Her face went slack. Another click and the watermelon was clearly in retreat. The player watched it, frowning, goose pimples blooming across her skin. She glanced quickly over her shoulder to see if anyone had noticed that the machine had malfunctioned. The top of the winning third pineapple dawned in the window.

Nedly could almost hear her heart beating; she kept looking away as though she wanted to run, but her eyes were drawn back to the windows as the third wheel nudged backwards and finally clicked into place. Three in a row. She held her breath; Nedly held his. There was a moment where time itself seemed to stand still and then in a torrent of electronic noise the machine started gushing coins, a waterfall of money dropping from the mouth of the machine and piling onto the floor until the machine was empty. The woman blinked, then, as she came to her senses, dropped to her knees and began scooping the coins into a pouch she made by holding on to the hem of her skirt.

From the back of the machine, Nedly beamed at her.

The sound of a big pay-out drew an instant crowd. Nedly turned to make an exit but people had gathered behind the machine, on all sides of it, craning their necks to see, jostling to get into the space where rogue coins might have rolled so they could lay their feet on them, and so he kept very still among the cogs and wires.

A figure in a black velvet tux with an amethyst-encrusted wreath around his grey curls began to descend the stairs from the high-roller tables. Two centurions joined him. The man in the tux whispered something to them and one peeled off towards the lobby while the other accompanied him across the floor.

'Psst! Hey!' Nedly tried to call out to the player, but of course she couldn't hear him. The crowd had jostled closer, penning them both in. She tried to stagger to her feet, cradling her winnings to stop the skirt material from splitting.

The man in the tux caught up with her. 'Congratulations, my dear, congratulations!' He took hold of her wrist firmly and raised it in the air in triumph, and a shower of coins rained out of her skirt. 'Who says these machines don't pay out? You've all seen it here with your own eyes!' He gave the centurion a meaningful look and he took hold of her other elbow. More coins fell to the floor. 'What's your name, my dear?'

'Ariman,' she whispered. Her eyes were darting now; her smile was wary.

'Carrie Ann!' he bellowed. 'Give her a big hand, everyone.' The room erupted into envious applause. 'Now then, let's take you out to the bank, get these heavy coins changed into crisp notes – what do you say to that, everyone?' He slammed her hard on the back and she dropped more coins.

'Then we can help you out to your car.'

'I don't have a car,' she protested. The second

centurion took the owner's place at her side and between him and his fellow security guard they lifted her off her feet and propelled her towards the back room.

'Looks like luck was on her side!' the man in the tux yelled. 'Next time it could be on yours!' He bared his teeth in a blindingly white grin, stretched out his arms, fingers wide as though he owned the room and everyone in it and then he made his exit, clapping heartily as he backed away.

The crowd cheered and surged round the machines and Nedly was stranded.

A wiry young man with his arm in plaster approached. He stared at the three wheels stuck on pineapples and Nedly stared back at him. The man's expression grew peaky.

A woman at the next machine along said, 'You're wasting your time: it's empty now. Didn't you see?'

But the man continued to stare, mesmerised. 'There's something weird about this one.' Nedly slunk back as carefully as he could. 'In fact,' the man said slowly, 'this whole place feels kind of . . . creepy.'

Nedly froze.

A woman in the row behind shuddered suddenly. 'Now that you mention it . . .' The colour drained out of her face. 'You don't think –?'

Nedly sank down to the floor and started crawling on his knees, backwards along the corridor of slots, trying to find the exit like a mouse caught in a maze, while around him panic had started to spread.

Someone did a blood-curdling scream, making Nedly jump. The lights started flickering and the crowd surged towards the entrance way, shoving each other and then shrieking when they mistook sharp elbows for the touch of a spectral hand.

A loud beaky voice suddenly cut through the noise. One by one the machines fell quiet as everyone turned to look the same way. Nedly clambered to his feet and followed their gaze to the figures in white hazmat suits with reflective orange visors striding up the purple carpet. There was a beat, a pause of silence and then panic broke out. The crowd split into those trying to leave and those trying to hide. The high rollers fled the tables, pouring down the stairs and into the lobby.

Ghostcatcher cut through the crowd like a harpoon through water. When they reached the end of the carpet they unhooked their laser consoles and activated them.

Nedly watched, paralysed with terror, unable to make his legs do anything until he saw the green light blinking, and then he ran. Up to the high-roller room, straight through baize blackjack tables and roulette wheels, through sequined dresses and shiny tuxedos, through screams and sweat and chip counters and wall after wall, through storage rooms filled with barrels, dark rooms with low-hanging lights and men in crumpled suits where smoke hung in the air, through carports and an alleyway, a warehouse, a subway.

Scene after scene streamed past in a blur of

shadows and all the time he could feel the heat of the green blinking light behind him, right at his heels, snapping hungrily, while in his mind's eye he tried to fix on Lil. Pushing everything else aside he focused as hard as he could on where she was at that moment. Then, with no more than a pop and a crackle in the air, Nedly Stubbs vanished.

Chapter 11

Undercover Baker

The next day the *Herald* ran the story.

> ### No dice for the Final Ghost
> *The fearless scientists of Ghostcatcher Inc.*
> *treated customers to a spectacular light*
> *show downtown last night in a close*
> *encounter with the Final Ghost.*
>
> *The ghost was trying to get its hands on*
> *Peligan City's riches at the jewel in the crown*
> *of the Golden Loop: the Wheel of Fortune!*

Casino owner Ray Jepetto said, 'Our patrons work hard, night and day at the slots, and this spook thinks it can walk into my joint and frighten them out of their winnings.'

The Final Ghost, who had earlier caused a slot machine to malfunction as well as creeping out casino guests, soon fled when Ghostcatcher unleashed their powerful laser net.

A witness from the Wheel of Fortune Security Team told the Herald, *'I dare the spook to show its face in the Loop again. If I get one iota of a hunch it's back, I'm going to crush it into a ball, dip it in concrete and throw it in the river, so to speak.'*

Sounds good to us!

Sheltering in the recessed double doorway at the back of Binky's Bagels, a boutique bakery on the edge of the plaza, Lil screwed the damp newspaper up into a ball and threw it angrily into a nearby bin.

She shook her head at Nedly. 'That could have been it, you know? The. End.'

Nedly curled his shoulders in and shuddered. 'For a moment I thought it was.'

'You've got to be smarter than that. You're supposed to be lying low.'

'I just wanted to do something good. I thought if I did then maybe people would think differently about me. I know it backfired but . . .' He ran out of words to explain with.

Lil looked across at him, all stooped and miserable, leaning into the doorway as though he hoped it could swallow him up. She couldn't knock him for trying. 'Forget about it,' she said. 'It was a fine idea. It's just, we ought to stick together – so I can watch your back. We have to be careful.'

'You mean *I* have to be careful.' Nedly rustled up a half-hearted grin. 'All right.' He turned to face Lil with his back to the wall. 'What are we doing here?'

Lil pulled out a pencil and started chewing on it. 'The way I see it we can't stay on the defensive. Ghostcatcher are getting too fast for us. We need to pull the plug on the whole enterprise and the neatest fix I can think of is to convince Gordian to stop funding them, right?'

'Right,' Nedly said, nodding.

'As it stands Ghostcatcher is costing the city big, but no one is even questioning it because they're all so scared of the so-called Final Ghost. Why?' She twiddled her pencil impressively between three fingers and then answered her own question. 'Because of that.' She pointed towards the bin.

Nedly started nodding and then paused uncertainly. 'The bin?'

'The casino story in the *Herald*,' Lil explained. 'As long as Sam Tangiers is stoking up the fear, people will think that getting the Final Ghost out of Peligan City is money well spent, so if the whole thing died down, then . . .' She raised her eyebrows. 'If the story goes away, then so does the funding.'

'So, you're going to stop the story?'

Lil attempted to conjure a steely look into her eyes. 'That's right. I'm going right to the top. Me and Sam Tangiers are going to have this out, reporter to reporter. I'm going to explain how he's got it all wrong about the Final Ghost.'

Nedly's eyes lit up. 'You're going to tell him that I'm one of the good guys?'

Lil glanced away. 'I'm probably going to have to play it by ear.'

'How are we going to get to him?'

'I've got a plan.' She turned to the doors, took hold of the handle and hesitated. When she turned back her expression was grave. 'You should sit this one out, somewhere safe,' she added.

Nedly's cheeks turned grey and his eyes darkened. 'I thought we were sticking together.'

Lil winced. 'We are. It's just . . . I was hoping you would be the lookout – in case any trouble comes my way.'

'O–K.'

'Great.' Lil started to tuck her hair behind

her ears but then fluffed it out again quickly when she realised they were probably luminous red. 'Keep your eyes and ears open and, Nedly, whatever happens, just keep a low profile.'

According to Minnie, a custard donut and an assortment of iced fancies was delivered to the editor's office at 11 a.m. every day.

Lil opened the back door of the bakery and snuck in. She picked up a white jacket from the hooks in the hallway and slipped it on. It was extra large, but, rolling up the sleeves as best she could, she took the cap out of the pocket and pulled it low over her eyes. Then she darted through to the delivery bay, found the white paper bag labelled up for Tangiers and stole it.

Across the road, on the other side of the plaza, stood the mighty greystone rectangle of the Tarbell Building, which housed the *Herald* offices. It looked like it had been woven out of concrete, a crosshatched façade over a multitude of small dark windows. It had been a feature of the city centre for more than fifty years but recently there had been a couple of new additions: a lift shaft — a long tube of toughened glass up the outside of the building; large brass letters, spelling out 'The Herald', and behind them a giant metallic fist clutching a rolled-up newspaper. It was easy to miss the words that had been carved into the stone above it, words that someone had tried to sandblast out of existence, but they were still there if you looked closely: words that read 'The Chronicle' – Peligan City's newspaper before it was shut down because its reporters started asking the wrong questions.

As far as Lil knew, this would be the first time a *Klaxon* reporter had crossed the threshold of the *Herald* news building since it had opened. This was enemy territory now.

Nedly was waiting by the glass porch, his eyes trained on the door.

'You look like a melting snowman.' He grinned at her.

Lil caught sight of her reflection; she had

forgotten to take off her rucksack so she had a humpback underneath her white coat. 'Come on, we've only got a few minutes before the real delivery person turns up.'

She stepped smartly into the revolving door, leaving a sweaty handprint on the smoked glass. Nedly hopped into the segment behind. In the lobby a portly security guard was sitting behind the fake marble counter with a copy of the morning's *Herald* spread out before her. She had frizzy blonde hair and raised brown-pencilled eyebrows.

Lil stood awkwardly in the middle of the lobby waiting for Nedly to join her. He had missed his moment to step out and had been stranded in his segment. The momentum of the door slowed down and then stopped, trapping him. He gave her a helpless shrug and yelled, 'I'll catch you up!'

'Just pass through the glass,' Lil muttered through gritted teeth.

The guard heaved her eyes off the page and weighed Lil with them. Lil flashed a trustworthy smile as Nedly started trying to press the door forward inch by inch, and held up the bag, 'Morning,' she said brightly. 'Delivery for –' she looked at the name on it as if for the first time – 'Tangiers.'

The guard's gaze flickered towards the doors that were slowly rotating on their own.

'I'm from the bakery,' Lil said, strolling nearer.

The guard dropped her brows flat in a frown. 'You're new and you're early.'

'First day on the job.' Lil shoved her long sleeves back up her arms and tipped the peak of her cap. 'Hoping to make a good impression.'

Nedly was almost free of the doors when someone stepped into another segment and they suddenly revolved at speed, squishing through him as he tried to exit. He reeled out with a queasy 'Gah!'. Lil grinned fixedly at the guard, who finally buzzed the button on her desk.

Nedly joined Lil with a *phew!* just as the lift doors opened.

As they rose smoothly above the building

line they watched the Golden Loop shrink away beneath them, its kaleidoscope of colours rippling wearily in the mid-morning gloom. Beyond it the grey blocks of downtown Peligan levelled out as they spread towards the river, until the only thing that broke the skyline was the shiny black column of City Hall, the tallest building in town, as it punched up through the concrete like a fist.

Lil shuddered at the sight of it. But Nedly said, 'I bet the city looks amazing from up there,' and pointed at its roof, and they both stood hypnotised for a moment until the lift glided to a stop.

Chapter 12

Sam Tangiers

The lift doors opened and Lil and Nedly stepped out into a tiled atrium where a wizened old man was polishing the floor to a treacherous shine.

'Act natural,' whispered Lil. Nedly raised his eyebrows in an *I'm invisible* kind of way and Lil nodded. 'I know. I'm just nervous.'

She walked briskly towards the glossy black door at the end of the room, her boots squeaking and trailing a fine dusting of flour behind her.

At the threshold they exchanged glances and Lil murmured, 'You wait here, keep an eye on things.' She knocked briskly.

Nedly opened his eyes extra wide and swivelled them. 'Trust me, OK, I know what I'm doing.'

'Come in,' a voice yelled and Lil pushed the door open.

The room was flashy, carpeted in a thick silvery pile. Sam Tangiers sat behind a chrome and black glass-topped desk in a generous red-leather swivel chair. He wore a bow tie with his pinstripe suit, his hair slicked to one side like a brown satin curtain and a widow's peak that would have looked good on a vampire. His eyebrows were the same size and shape as his eyes, like two dark smudges on his forehead.

He was signing off a wad of papers with a gold-plated ball-point pen. Lil crossed the room in silence and placed the bag down on the desk next to a large marbled paperweight. The bag had grown stickier and more crumpled-looking on the way over.

Tangiers frowned at it and then glanced up at her. 'You're not the usual delivery boy.'

'No, he's sick.'

He pulled the bag towards him and peered inside. Lil didn't move. He looked up. 'Are you waiting for a tip?'

Lil raised her chin. 'No. Actually, I have a tip for you and I'm not a delivery boy at all – or a delivery girl.' She cut him off before he could correct her. 'I'm a reporter.' She Squinted at him from under the cap.

He eyed her with distaste. 'Do you work for me?'

'No!' Lil snorted. Tangiers' hand went wearily to the security buzzer on the underside of his desk. 'Wait! It's about the Final Ghost!'

He pressed it anyway. 'Are you looking for a job?'

'No!' Lil hissed through gritted teeth. 'Not in a million years. I came here to tell you something about the Final Ghost.'

Tangiers sighed. 'Phone it in to the tip line.' He went back to signing the papers. 'We've got operators taking down stories night and day.'

'But I have inside information.'

'Who doesn't? Stories about the Final Ghost are ten a penny.' The telephone lit up. Tangiers pressed the button and picked up the receiver 'Sports desk? OK – did Peligan City win?'

He frowned down the line. 'No? Hide it at the back. Anything else? Tiddlywinks? What's that?' His face soured while he listened. 'All right, go with the tiddlywinks. Puff it up with the history of the game and all that, run the other side down. What was the prize? That's all? Double it.' He slammed the phone down.

'Hey! Tangiers,' Lil tried again.

'Are you looking for an apprenticeship?'

'No!' Lil shouted louder than she meant to.

Tangiers ignored her. 'Here.' He opened a drawer and pulled out a picture of himself sitting at the same desk he was sitting at now, holding the pen over a notebook, pretending to have just looked up. He signed it and slid it across to her. 'There you go – now scram.'

Lil ignored the picture.

Tangiers took the custard donut out of the bag and grimaced at it. It must have been in the bit of the bag that Lil had been holding. It hung limply from his fingers and then dropped to the desktop with a pale yellow plop. He pressed another button on his phone and snapped into it, 'Get down to Binky's, have someone fired and fetch me a new donut.'

A squeaky voice replied, 'Right away, Mr Tangiers.'

'And find out what's keeping security – I've got some kind of obsessive fan here that needs to be shown the door.' He pressed the receiver button down five or six times impatiently and then, pointedly ignoring Lil, he dialled, cramming an iced fancy into his mouth and chewing while he waited. 'Weather desk?' he said with his mouth full. 'Make it light, a shower at best – people are sick of rain, it's all we get.'

The phone lit up again, and he pushed the button. 'Bury it.' Another button lit.

He shook his head. 'Run it anyway.'

'Look –' Lil began.

Tangiers looked at her like she was a fly he'd found floating in his drink. 'You're still here? Security is on their way.' He flapped the signed photograph at her again.

The phone lit up and this time Lil pushed all the buttons down. 'I came here to talk to you and I'm not leaving until you listen.'

Tangiers sighed theatrically and looked at his watch. 'All right, you have my attention for one minute.' He pulled a chamois cloth out from his desk drawer and began buffing his fingernails with it. 'What makes you think you should have a job at the *Herald*?'

Lil balled her hands into fists and squeezed them 'til they shook. Then she took a deep breath. 'I came here to talk to you about the Final Ghost. You need to know that you've got it wrong. About the ghost. All of it.' Her eyes flickered over to the door and she gulped. 'There is no Final Ghost. It's a hoax.'

Tangiers laughed to himself and jabbed at

177

the security button again. 'If there's no Final Ghost, then tell me who's been scaring our sports teams out of winning, terrorising the streets, stalking people at night. Creeping into their bedrooms and hiding in their mirrors, spooking their pets, giving children nightmares, turning milk sour –'

Lil cut him off. 'No one is doing any of that stuff. You're just making it up.'

There was a knock at the door. 'Security,' a voice said. The knob turned but the door wouldn't open. 'Could you unlock the door please, Mr Tangiers?'

'It's not locked!' Tangiers bellowed.

Nedly stuck his head and shoulders through the door. 'Lil! He called Security!'

Lil tried to nod him away.

'I slowed them down.' Nedly extricated himself from the glossy black wood with a *squerp*. 'How's it going?'

The temperature in the office cooled by a couple of degrees and Tangiers darted a look over his shoulder. 'You want me to drop the best story we've ever run because the Final Ghost doesn't really exist? That's what you wanted to ask me?' He smirked at her. 'Why exactly would I want to do that?'

'Lil?' said Nedly.

Lil pointed an accusing finger at Tangiers. 'You're frightening people.'

'People love being scared,' the editor laughed nastily. 'They wouldn't buy the paper if they didn't.' A dusting of sugar outlined his mouth and he wiped it away with a Binky's serviette.

Lil persisted. 'They think they're getting the news.'

That made him laugh so much that tears came to his eyes. 'No they don't. Not really. The public just loves a good ghost story! *Herald* sales are up one hundred and fifty per cent since the Final Ghost.' He tutted to himself. 'The Final Ghost – whoever came up with that name ought to be fired.' He pressed the button on his phone and snapped into it, 'Steve, memo to the staff writers: come up with a scarier name than the Final Ghost. Scariest name gets a prize.'

'What did you tell him?' Nedly's lips were tight and thin.

Lil shook her head firmly, and gave him a look that said, *Let me handle this*.

Tangiers replaced the handset and said, 'Now, I admire your moxie, little girl, but I've got important work to do so you'll have to excuse me. I've got the news to report.'

Lil stuck her heels into the carpet. 'This isn't the news.'

He snorted at her. 'It's in a newspaper, isn't it? Are you sure you're from Binky's Bagels?'

'No, I already told you I'm not. If you had bothered to investigate, you would know that the serious crime rate has actually fallen over the last few weeks.'

Tangiers beamed at her. 'We don't need to investigate; we get our news straight from the cops. They tell us what happens and we print it.' He picked up another fancy.

The door rattled as the security guards attempted to force it open.

One called out respectfully. 'Mr Tangiers, the door still seems to be locked.'

'I haven't locked it –' Tangiers began and then he turned to Lil, his eyes narrowed. 'What are you playing at?'

'Nothing to do with me,' said Lil but when her eyes met Nedly's she saw they were glowering.

The buzzer on the desk rang, 'Yes! Hello?' There was no one there. He put the phone down. It rang again. Tangiers shook it and tapped the receiver. It rang again before he had replaced the handset. He moaned. 'This thing is broken!' The lights on the phone started flashing one by one.

Nedly was glaring at him. Tangiers picked up the phone. 'Can you get an engineer up here? Hello? Hello? It's dead.' Lil flicked Nedly a warning glance.

Tangiers had broken out into a cold sweat. 'Do you feel that?' he asked Lil. 'Look, I realise

you're young, you've got ideals – well done for that, it's very sweet. But this is going beyond a joke and you've taken up enough of my time.'

Lil could see the sweat beading on his top lip, as he dismissed her with a flick of his wrist and returned to signing the ream of papers, pretending she wasn't there.

Nedly sat down on the corner of his desk. Tangiers' signature became shaky so he put down his pen. All the buttons on the phone lit up and he nervously picked up the receiver. A thin, ghostly howl came down the line.

'Hello?' he gasped and then blanched and threw the handset away from him. Tangiers staggered to his feet, then collapsed backwards again.

A chair scooted suddenly across the floor and wedged itself under the door handle.

'What the . . . ?' Tangiers turned a shade of grey. He looked wildly at Lil. 'What are you doing?' He made a grab for her mac but she ducked out of his way.

All the sheets of paper on the desk flew up in turn, and hung in the air above them.

'Stop this now!' he snarled fearfully.

A freezing draught prickled all the hairs on Lil's neck. 'No,' she pleaded. 'Not like this.'

Goose pimples rose on Tangier's skin and his anger drained away, leaving a fear that was as hollow as a disused well. His breath billowed in a cloud in front of him. 'Hello?' he whispered. 'Is . . . anybody there?' His gold pen started spinning on his desk, revolving into a blur.

'The Final Ghost is real?' he whispered. His voice had a strangled tone, his eyes quivered bloodshot and his face turned grey.

The marble paperweight started orbiting the gold pen; the smoked-glass desktop cracked.

'You're making it worse!' yelled Lil.

Nedly's eyes were dark and stormy.

The papers fluttered around the room like birds caught in a cyclone. Lil crawled under the desk and crouched there with her hands over her head, while the spectral wind grew until it raged through the suite, pulling in ornaments from every surface and then propelling them out to hammer against the external glass wall.

'Please! NEDLY!' she shouted. 'Stop! STOP!'

The papers fell to floor. Lil opened her eyes. Tangiers was passed out in his custard donut, and Nedly was gone.

Chapter 13

The Drop

That afternoon Lil and Abe took cover from the rain under the shelter of the bandstand while Margaret followed her nose in figures of eight round the base of a threadbare old shrub. Nedly wandered at a distance, pretending to look for a stick to throw, hands stuffed in his pockets.

The floor of the bandstand was plastered in decaying leaves and rubbish. Lil leant on the railings and looked up at the filigree of wrought-iron that webbed the pillars and then turned her Penetrating Squint on the surrounding grass.

'Why do you think Starkey wants to meet us here, out in the open?'

Abe shrugged. 'Search me.'

'I don't trust him.' She beckoned Nedly closer. 'Stick with us. This could be a trap.'

Reluctantly Nedly joined them. 'Is it too much to hope that someone might actually be on our side for once? Starkey warned us about Ghostcatcher, didn't he? He told you I was in danger and that's why you came to find me at the boxing club.'

'And then Ghostcatcher turned up.' Lil raised her eyebrows. 'So, how did he know they were coming? How did he even know you were there?'

'If he wasn't on our side, why would he have told us about the delivery?'

Lil gave the end of her pencil a good chew and then spat out some wood. 'Maybe to lure us.'

'You're being paranoid.'

'And you're not paranoid enough. Listen, Nedly, the whole of Peligan City is against you – we can't take any risks, and after this morning . . .'

'I know!' Nedly yelled. 'I made it worse!'

Lil was taken aback by the outburst, but gave him a one-shouldered shrug. 'We both did. But it was my fault; it was a stupid idea anyway. I just thought it was worth a shot.'

Nedly glanced sideways at her. 'I think Starkey is worth a shot.'

'Fine.' Lil gave up; she was sick of arguing. 'But stay close, in case it is a trap, in which case –'

'In which case, run. I know.' He rolled his eyes at her but in a jokey way.

A figure in a leaf-green poncho suddenly emerged from a nearby bush, looked left and right and then darted up the steps, slipped on the leaves and fell to the floor at their feet with a yelp.

'I see we're keeping a low profile.' Abe held

out his left hand to help Starkey up. Starkey made a grab for the right at the same time and pulled the prosthetic off. It fell amongst the rubbish onto the floor.

'My gods!' said Starkey, staring at it. The fingertips were spoon-shaped from when they had melted slightly and the surface was grey with soot. It looked like the hand of a corpse.

'It's OK,' said Lil. 'It's not a real hand.'

'It's very . . . lifelike,' Starkey complimented Abe, still staring at the dismembered appendage. He was no longer wearing his glasses and his eyes were wide and feverish-looking.

Margaret bounded up the steps and jumped playfully at Starkey just as he tried to stand. He fell back down again, laughing and ruffling her fur.

Nedly watched enviously.

'So,' said Lil. 'What is it you wanted to tell us?'

'Ah yes.' Starkey stumbled to his feet. His poncho was decorated in dead leaves. He took up a post by the railings. 'Good morning, all of you.' He looked terrified for a minute. 'I'm not standing on him, am I?'

Lil stuck out her chin. 'Who says he's here? It's not exactly safe for him out in the open.'

Starkey winced. 'Quite right, of course. I must not endanger our friend. Not for a moment. I thought you would prefer to meet somewhere quiet, but you're right.' He looked at them soberly. 'I'm not sure anywhere is really safe now.'

'So, what gives?' Abe planted his feet solidly in the centre of the bandstand.

'I have some information,' Starkey whispered, glancing over his shoulder. 'I have discovered what Ghostcatcher are using the tourmaline for.'

Lil and Nedly drew in.

'They are feeding it to EGON.'

Lil pulled a grim face and looked askance at Starkey and then Abe. 'Who's EGON?'

'Not who, what,' Starkey replied. 'EGON is an Electromagnetic Geospatial Orientation Network.'

'Sounds impressive,' said Abe, cloaking his bewilderment in cynicism. 'What does it actually do?'

'It finds ghosts.'

'Like those camera things Ghostcatcher have been using? The EMF readers?' asked Lil.

Starkey creased his brow slightly. 'On a larger scale. Much larger. EGON finds ghosts in the city. Wherever they are.'

Lil gulped. 'The whole city?'

'Every corner.'

She tried to catch Nedly's eye. His face was ice-white.

'That's why they needed so much tourmaline,' Starkey continued, his breath billowing like mist in the suddenly freezing atmosphere of the bandstand. 'They have spent the last few weeks calibrating it to the exact frequency emitted by the Final Ghost. They had a few false positives but now they're confident that EGON can track the ghost wherever it is in Peligan City. They are primed for its capture and destruction.'

The wind picked up and pulled the leaves off the ground and rolled them a few paces. The bare trees swayed, like seaweed being tugged by an underwater current. 'I thought you should know what you're up against.'

Lil shuddered and then gave him the Squint. 'How do you know so much about it?'

'Because I've seen it!' Starkey's voice broke excitedly. 'The night after we met. When another shipment came in I stowed away in the truck and was delivered into the Rorschach Laboratory Facility. Do you know it?'

'We've heard of it,' Abe and Lil said at the same time.

'As soon as the truck parked I crawled out from beneath the tarpaulin.'

'You broke in?' The scowl Lil had been wearing softened slightly.

'I did. The security round the perimeter is very high but inside the camp it's just tents. Very thin walls,' he chuckled. 'I hid out for the best part of the evening listening to them scanning the city. I procured some branches from an overgrown shrubbery and with my green poncho I was completely camouflaged as a bush.' He demonstrated by puffing out the poncho and crouching onto his knees. When he bowed his head his face disappeared and he became a strange canvas boulder. 'I was planning to escape by secreting myself in the back of the Ghostcatcher van but unfortunately I was discovered.

'A call came in on the Haunting Hotline and, in their hurry to answer it, the scientists stumbled upon me in my hiding place, quite literally. They called the police, and then one of them was kind enough to make small talk with me until the authorities arrived.'

Abe narrowed his eyes. 'That was very sociable, seeing as how you were trespassing.'

'That way I had a good look at EGON.' Starkey's eyes glistened. 'It's an impressive machine. I even found out a little about how it works.' He lowered his voice to a whisper again. 'That's when I realised the danger, though I didn't have a chance to warn you until the next morning when the police allowed me to make a phone call.'

Lil nodded, remembering the call she had taken at the Nite Jar. But she still wasn't convinced. 'Then they just let you go?'

'I have a suspicion that they think I'm a bit nutty,' he confessed. He raised his eyes to Lil. 'I got away with a caution.'

'Ghostcatcher thinks they have us cornered,' said Lil, remembering Virgil's ninety-nine per cent. She looked anxiously at Nedly.

Abe clenched and unclenched his jaw and then punched his open rubber hand menacingly with his real one. 'I'd like to bust that EGON's swede.'

Starkey nodded excitedly. 'That's the other thing I wanted to tell you. I think we could destroy it.'

Abe hesitated mid-punch. 'How?'

Starkey looked down at Margaret and then followed her gaze to the empty space by the steps. 'I believe the Final Ghost could do it, with a surge of electromagnetic energy.'

'Lil?' Nedly spoke for the first time since Starkey had arrived. 'Will you tell him my name? I don't want to be the Final Ghost.' He held her uncertain gaze for a moment. 'Please.'

Reluctantly Lil turned to Starkey. 'His name is Nedly, that's what you should call him.'

Starkey's eyes brimmed as he repeated the word. 'Nedly. You can communicate with him?'

She nodded. Starkey raised his eyebrows at Abe, who shook his head.

'As far as we know she's the only one who can.'

'Is it some kind of sixth sense or a natural sensitivity to ghosts?'

'Nedly is the only ghost I can see.' Lil shrugged.

Starkey frowned. 'Have you any idea why that is?'

Lil chewed on her pencil and looked at Nedly, who looked at the floor. 'Honestly, I haven't got a clue.'

Chapter 14

Old Towels

Lil sat alone in one of the booths that lined the far wall of the Nite Jar Cafe, eating her tea and reading that evening's edition of the *Klaxon*, hidden inside yesterday's edition of the *Herald*. A familiar shadow flooded the table and then slipped away as its owner lurched into the seat opposite.

'Abe,' Lil said with a grin.

'Lil,' he returned the greeting and then paused

to let his eyes and ears read the atmosphere. 'No Nedly?'

Lil shook her head. 'He's trailing Starkey to see if he's on the level.'

'Is that a good idea?' Abe frowned. 'If he's not, then he could be dangerous.'

'That's what I said.' Lil stabbed a piece of cheese on toast. 'But he's gone anyway.'

'You two had a bust-up?'

She shrugged.

'Don't take it personally; the world is on his shoulders right now.' He nodded at her plate. 'What have you got there?'

'It's a signature dish that Yoshi has been working on.'

'Any good?'

Lil cut a corner and offered it to him. Abe accepted it and chewed a couple of times, then his face curdled. 'What's that on the cheese? Some kind of fruit?'

'It's pineapple,' she grimaced. 'Yoshi thought I would like it. I don't want to hurt his feelings but it's the most terrible combination I've ever tasted. Will you help me eat it?'

They both looked at the counter where Yoshi was mashing up some leftover eggs and bacon for Margaret. He grinned back at them and gave them a thumbs up. Abe took the knife and cut the toasted cheese down the middle. 'All right, kid. We're in it together.'

He tapped the *Klaxon*. 'Anything in there we should know about?'

Lil raised a Cryptic Eyebrow. 'Ghostcatcher have opened a new line of enquiry.'

Ghostcatcher Awarded New Powers to Search and Destroy 'haunted objects' by Marsha Quake

In a joint operation with City Hall, Ghostcatcher have been authorised to Search and Destroy suspicious items as they pursue a second line of enquiry: where is the object that the Final Ghost has been bound to and who is controlling it?

In an exclusive interview with the Klaxon,

lead scientist Magdalena Virgil explains: 'Our investigations have concluded that all the ghosts haunting Peligan City were bound to objects, and this is the means by which they were controlled.

'Without something to anchor them, the ghosts certainly wouldn't be able to manifest to the extent that they could haunt anyone, and so we have deduced that if the object is destroyed then the associated ghost should also perish.'

Acting Mayor Gordian has advised that anyone found in possession of a haunted object could face criminal charges and they are asking the public to be vigilant of people acting suspiciously around material goods.

Peligan City Police Department reserves the right to destroy any object viewed as haunted.

But if this theory is well founded, then why are we only hearing about it now? Or is this an attempt to reinvigorate a crusade

that the public interest and city purse are
growing weary of?

'They've got it all wrong,' said Lil, chewing
and grimacing in turn. 'Nedly's not like the
other spooks. He wasn't bound to anything.'

'Suits us.' Abe rubbed his chin. 'If they're
looking for something that isn't there, it will
keep them busy anyway.' He took a bite of the
toasted cheese and pineapple and winced.
'Quake got exclusive action on this – didn't she
ask you along?'

'She did,' Lil admitted. 'There was something
else I had to do, to try to fix things. I thought
if I could persuade Sam Tangiers . . .' Abe's
jaw dropped but before he could speak Lil cut
him off: 'It was a terrible idea, I know that
now.' She sighed miserably. 'It's beginning to
feel like we're running out of options.'

Abe ate another two mouthfuls of toasted
cheese without balking. He had something even
more bad-tasting in his mouth and it was past
time to spit it out. He looked at Lil for a

moment and then started playing with the lever on the napkin dispenser. 'You know, with EGON on the scene, it might be time for Nedly to . . . move on.'

'What!' Lil choked.

'Somewhere people don't know him,' Abe continued carefully. 'Not for ever, just until they get tired of looking.'

'Nedly leave Peligan City?' The magnitude of the suggestion bowled Lil over. 'But this is his home.'

'I know it's not what you want to hear but you have to face up to it; this has just got too big for us to handle. We can't protect him, not against the whole city and all that science. Lil . . . you've got to think about your future. The rest of your life.'

Lil gave him a look. 'What about Nedly's life? I'm not just going to throw in the towel when he needs me.' There was an accusing look in her eye.

Abe took that on the chin. 'Take it from someone who's knee-deep in old towels.' He looked at Lil steadily. 'Look where it got me. I was chasing Le Teef for ten years, going round in circles. Don't be stubborn like me.'

'You got him in the end.'

They both chewed on doggedly and in silence, and then finally Lil said: 'I'm not ready to give up and I've got another idea now anyway. Do you know what Mum thinks about the Final Ghost? She doesn't believe he exists.'

'So I've heard.' Abe poured them both a glass of water from the jug and drank his in two glugs. 'She makes a good case for it too.'

Lil pulled her jumper sleeves down over her hands; it felt chilly in the Nite Jar – she glanced at the door, but it was closed. 'So, I was thinking, if I worked on her a bit, maybe the *Klaxon* could run a story about the Final Ghost not being real. Quake would confirm that Ghostcatcher haven't seen any verifiable action over the last few weeks. Mum could get hold of the records from the Police Department to confirm the serious crime rate has fallen. I think it would hang together.' Lil pulled the pencil out of her hair and chewed on it pensively.

Abe creased his brow. 'But you know it isn't true.'

'Yeah, I know, but if people buy it, they'll leave Nedly alone. He'll be safe.'

'Yeah but nothing,' Abe growled. 'That's a road you do not want to walk down. If you're going to start making up stories when it suits you, maybe you should go and work for the *Herald*.'

His words caught Lil like a stinger. 'That's not what I meant,' she bristled, and then muttered angrily, 'You don't know anything about it. You're just an old gumshoe.'

Abe stared down at his rubber hand and busied himself with squeezing the end of each of the fingers in turn. 'I know a little something about how it feels to not be able to look yourself in the eye.'

Lil took the last bite of cheese and pineapple. It was hard to swallow.

'It's got really cold in here,' she grumbled,

scowling at the radiator. Goose pimples bloomed on her skin and then her stomach turned to ice. She stood up on the seat and looked over into the next booth.

'Nedly!' Lil's ears burned red. 'How long have you been there?'

'Long enough.' His skin looked like the surface of a frozen lake.

'Were you spying on me?' Lil gave him the Squint, full blast.

Nedly glared back at her. 'When were you actually going to tell me about your big plan to pretend that I don't even exist, or don't I get a say in it?'

Lil could feel her heartbeat thumping in her chest. She started to get some serious creeps but she couldn't make herself back down – in fact, the creepier she felt, the angrier she got. 'Don't try and creep me out!' she yelled.

'Don't tell me what to do!' Nedly yelled back.

'Shhh!' Abe hissed between gritted teeth while smiling awkwardly to the people sitting at the counter who had turned round to stare at Lil. 'Sit down, will you?'

The tension in the air was thick enough to slice. 'All right, kids,' he whispered hoarsely, cold sweat beading on his brow. 'We're all on the same side here.' He held his hands out open-palmed. 'Let's sit down together, have something to drink to take away the memory of that . . . cheese and fruit, and work it out.'

Nedly circled round to take the seat opposite Lil, his eyes blazing. Lil glowered back at him. Abe shivered violently and took out his crumpled handkerchief and mopped his face with it. 'That's better. Now, it so happens I have a plan of my own.'

'You do?' Lil was so surprised that she broke her unblinking staring contest with Nedly. As she looked away Nedly's expression relaxed and by the time she looked back at him she saw what she had missed before: she had hurt his feelings. She gave him a small tentative smile, a peace offering.

'We'll do it together, with a bit of this.' Abe

tapped the side of his head. 'Brains.' He explained: 'For starters we're going to eliminate the immediate threat by taking EGON out of the game, which should buy us some thinking time at least.'

Nedly looked doubtful. 'But EGON is behind the security fence at Rorschach; how will we even get in there?'

Lil told him firmly, 'We'll find a way.'

'We already tried.' Nedly wilted with a sigh. 'There isn't a way.'

Lil thumped her fist on the table, making Abe jump. 'Nedly, look at me.' He bored his eyes into the floor and then reluctantly his gaze slid across to Lil's empty plate. 'In the eye,' she insisted. Nedly rolled his eyes up. 'Have you ever known me to give up on something I believe in?'

Nedly looked down at the plate again and shrugged.

Lil pushed it aside. 'Well, have you?'

He sighed. 'No.'

'That's right,' she said. 'And I'm not about to start now.'

A smile twitched at his lips. He looked from Abe to Lil and then back again. 'So, what is the plan?'

Lil glanced at Abe with a trace of desperation in her eyes.

'It's a classic,' he told them. 'They use it in all the pictures, and, let me tell you, it works every time.' He puffed himself up and turned to face the spot Lil had been talking to with confidence. 'The plan is that we're going to assemble a crack team, specialists in their field, and with their expertise we're going to out-think those eggheads, infiltrate the facility and locate the target . . . and –' he shrugged – 'bust EGON's swede.'

Lil nodded her head with caution. 'Right . . .' Nedly was watching her hopefully. 'That could work,' she added, sounding like she was warming to the idea. She had no idea how that was going to work, but at that moment they just needed something. 'First we need some plans, of the alarm system and the layout of the facility.' She paused. 'Where are we going to find something like that at this short notice?'

Abe rubbed his grizzled chin thoughtfully and then grinned. 'I suppose we'd have to know the sort of person who knows things.'

At the corner of Fig Street, Minnie's cart was bathed in the light of a street lamp. The steam from the grill billowed out like mist, carrying with it the smell of warm bread, onions and sausages as it drifted through the rain.

Minnie's face broke into a crooked smile when she saw them. 'Nearly every day, detective! This is becoming like old times. What can I get you – a couple of dogs?'

'No time for any food. What I'm looking for . . .' Abe tugged down the brim of his trilby and then glanced over his shoulder. '. . . are some plans to the grounds of the old asylum out at Rorschach.'

Minnie's smile dropped. 'What, no small talk?'

'No time.' Abe fixed her with his steely eye. 'Can you help?'

Minnie crossed her arms. 'Try the library.'

'The sort of plans we're looking for aren't on public record. We're particularly interested in the design plans for the security system around the perimeter wall. And anyway, the library's shut.'

'All sounds perfectly above board to me.' She gave him a cynical look.

'I've got some urgent business at that new research facility and I can't seem to get an invite.'

'I'm a hot dog seller. What makes you think I can lay my hands on that kind of material?'

Abe eyed her sternly. 'Minnie, what you don't know about Peligan City isn't worth knowing.'

She frowned back at him and dropped her voice. 'If I go looking for information like that, out of the blue and time-sensitive, it's going to cause a ripple –' She broke off suddenly. 'Hey, Lenny.'

A man in a long woollen coat and a military cap shuffled out from the shadows. He kept his head bent low and asked in a quiet voice, 'Got any throwaways, Minnie?'

Minnie's hard eyes softened. She surveyed the line of perfect bangers sizzling on the hotplate and then selected a fat one. 'Here, this fellow got a bit burnt on the side.' She dropped it in a bun for him. The man dipped his eyes gratefully as he turned. Minnie watched him go and the soft look had an edge of anger in it.

She kept her voice low. 'Look, detective, none of us are far from the gutter in this town. If I start asking too many questions, I might make things awkward for myself. Draw the wrong kind of attention.'

'You know what, Minnie?' Abe growled. 'Everyone's got something to lose, but sooner or later we're all going to have to stand up for what we believe in or move aside and let Peligan City slide into the mud.'

Minnie gave Abe a hard stare of her own and then dropped it with an I-should-know-better shake of her head. 'Tell you what, I'll lift up a few rocks, see what's under them. But just keep it on the down-low, right?' She sighed. 'See you tomorrow. If I can find anything, I'll have it by then.'

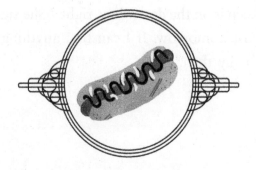

Chapter 15

The Team Works

The following afternoon the music in the Nite Jar had dropped tempo to a laid-back swing as Lil piled into the booth next to Nedly, and Abe took his seat opposite. Margaret got into position by his feet under the table. Yoshi was wiping the steam off the windows, the water spots he left behind catching the light from passing cars.

'So.' Lil laced her fingers together and flexed her arms. 'Who are we expecting – for the crack team?'

'Did I say crack team?' Abe rubbed his jaw with his rubber hand. 'I don't remember using those terms exactly.'

'Crack team of specialists,' Lil reminded him.

Abe puckered his lips out like a duck's bill. 'Well . . .'

There was a knock on the window and a face appeared, surrounded by the tight green hood of a waterproof poncho.. Yoshi jumped and cried out. Starkey's face fell. He ran quickly into the cafe, skidded on some wet footprints and lurched at Yoshi crying, 'I'm so sorry! What a numbskull!'

'It's fine,' said Yoshi, smiling.

'Good of you,' said Starkey, pumping Yoshi's hand, which still held the wet cloth.

'What can I get you?'

'I'm just here to meet up, with some . . . friends.' Starkey edged his way to the booth where Abe and Lil were sitting.

'Hello,' he said when he reached them, and slid in next to Abe.

There was a pause.

'Is this everyone?' Lil asked, trying not to sound disappointed.

'Hey, Mandrel!' Minnie came through the door and crossed the floor like a gunslinger slowly and with her gaze sliding from side to side to check who was where. She was wearing her trapper hat and gold hoop earrings and her jaw worked absent-mindedly over the gum she was chewing. Wisps of wet hair clung to the rain on her face. She was carrying something in her pocket and drew it out when she reached them. It was a hot dog bun.

She held the bun out to Abe and he took hold but Minnie didn't let go. 'Be careful, detective. I don't know what you've got yourself wrapped up in but –'

'We'll be fine,' Abe assured her, squidging the bun as he tried to extract it.

Minnie kept a tight hold. 'We go back a long way, Mandrel, and you've always been a good man.' Abe started to shrug. 'No, you have. A little shabby maybe, but . . . I still remember when they used to call you the Scourge of the Underworld.'

'That is a long way back.' Abe rubbed his grizzled chin.

'I know you've had a few knocks, but a few months back, when you helped take down Le Teef and exposed the corruption at City Hall –'

'Some of it,' Lil chipped in.

'Indeed. Reminded me of the old days. And then yesterday, there you were asking me for plans and details and I ask myself, is something big going down? Is Mandrel onto something?'

'It's just for a case I'm working on.'

Minnie nodded at Starkey. 'All of you?'

'It's a big case.'

Minnie nodded again. 'And what you were saying about people needing to step up and all that . . .'

'What do you want, Minnie?'

'I want in.' She slid into the booth next to Starkey, who squashed further into Abe. 'What's the plan?'

'You won't like it.' Lil took a steadying breath. 'So, before we tell you, you need to know that this is about protecting the Final Ghost. We're on his side.'

Minnie stopped chewing her gum and looked askance at Lil. 'You're going to tell me he's one of the good guys too – right?'

'The best,' said Lil, and she flicked a warm look at Nedly.

Minnie sighed. She took off her cap and rubbed some life into her auburn hair. 'You know, I was there that night at the Wheel of Fortune, when the Final Ghost struck. I was playing the slots.' She eyeballed Lil and Abe in turn. 'You didn't know that about me, did you? If it wasn't for that place I would have had myself a hot dog restaurant by now.' She smiled bitterly and gave her gum a good chew.

'Now in all my time at the Wheel I've never seen anyone beat the house, and they say that the Final Ghost was behind it. It looked to me like the ghost fixed that machine so the lady would get lucky for once. It looked to me like

maybe he was trying to do something good – not trying to spook people like everybody is saying.' Nedly's cheeks blushed a soft grey and his eyes shone.

'That got me thinking,' Minnie continued. 'I don't like the way things are run in this town, never have, and we all know that that *Herald* just prints whatever City Hall wants it to. Now, I can't say I'm a hundred per cent comfortable with the idea of a ghost here in Peligan, but if the *Herald* says that it's the enemy, then I'm inclined to believe the opposite, and now if you're saying the ghost is all right too . . .' She looked at Abe for reassurance and got it with a tilt of his head. '. . . then he's all right with me.' She shrugged and pulled her hat back on. 'When do I get to meet him?'

'How about now?' Lil caught Minnie's gaze and then used her eyes to point to the place where Nedly was sitting.

Minnie shivered involuntarily and her chewing gum fell out of her mouth. She put it back in quickly, looked at the empty space beside Lil and said, 'Pleased to meet you,' with a grin, then she shrugged her bodywarmer up with her shoulders and buried her chin in the neck of it.

Nedly raised his hand in a shy unseen wave.

'OK, so –' Abe and Lil said at the same time, then they both laughed.

Abe said, 'You go.'

Lil replied, 'No, you go. You've done this sort of thing before, right? When you were a police detective, special operations. And takedowns and missions . . . '

Abe tried to shrug it off bashfully and held up his rubber hand. 'I don't know about all that –'

Margaret laid a paw on his knee and looked faithfully up at him and Nedly gave him an encouraging smile that Abe couldn't see. Nevertheless he loosened his tie, cleared his throat, took a sip of water and began:

'OK.' He looked over his shoulder and as he leaned forward across the table, the others did too. 'So, as Lil was saying, this concerns our friend.' He nodded soberly to the corner where Nedly sat, his eyes darting a question to Lil just to be sure he was still definitely there.

Abe prised open the hot dog bun and pulled out the tightly rolled map inside it. He spread it out over the table and they all held a corner down with the tips of their fingers. 'Our friend is in trouble: everyone's scared of him and Ghostcatcher are closing in. They've developed some kind of technology to track him down and now time is running out before they catch up with him and . . . We're looking at a –' he dropped his voice – 'a covert operation out at the old asylum at Rorschach, which is where the Ghostcatcher facility is located. It houses a machine called EGON.'

'Electromagnetic Geospatial Orientation Network,' explained Starkey.

'That's what we need to destroy,' confirmed Lil.

'What are you lot whispering about?' said Velma as she put the tray down on the table.

Everyone scrambled to cover the map as they

reached onto the tray and started unloading the pot of coffee, glasses of milk and a huge plate of assorted pastries.

Velma narrowed her eyes at it. 'What's that you've got? Looks like some kind of map? You're not planning a robbery, are you?' They laughed, for slightly too long, and Starkey even pretended to wipe his eyes.

Velma stood waiting. 'Well?' she said finally.

'No way,' said Lil.

'We're just chewing the fat,' said Abe.

Velma held out her hand and the gang turned out their pockets to pool enough money together to cover the bill. She picked up the coins, muttering, 'Have it your own way,' and returned to the counter to watch them from behind the glass cake domes.

Abe continued, 'To get to EGON we need a clear run of the facility so we'll have to draw Ghostcatcher into the city and away from the old asylum. We need to trick them into a safe spot where we can control things. Somewhere familiar; public but not too public.'

They all thought hard and Lil looked up at Nedly and then at Velma at the counter. 'How about here?'

Yoshi and Velma pulled up seats. They looked at the space in the corner and didn't query why Lil hadn't budged up.

'The way it is,' Abe told them, 'we need you to lure someone to the Nite Jar, and then keep them here as long as possible.'

'Like a kidnapping?' Velma looked accusingly at Starkey. 'I don't know what this fellow has got you mixed up in but –'

'No, that sounded worse than it is,' said Lil. 'We just need a distraction and we wondered about here?'

'What kind of distraction?'

'We just need to bounce some electromagnetic energy around.'

'Will it damage the fittings?'

They all looked at Starkey and he shook his head, confidently at first and then less so.

Velma frowned but Yoshi said, 'Why?'

'To help out a friend.' Lil took a big gulp of milk.

Yoshi gave her a look. 'Does it have anything to do with that ghost that you hang around with?'

'Whaaat!' Lil sprayed the milk all across the map and then pulled handfuls of serviettes out of the dispenser and started blotting wildly. 'Why – why would you say that?'

Yoshi shrugged. 'I've just seen you talking to yourself, sometimes you buy two of something, and you always leave a seat free when you're here. Just like you have now. Velma thought maybe you just liked talking to yourself.' Velma nodded in confirmation. 'But I wondered if maybe there was more to it.'

Velma added, 'We don't read the *Herald* but we've both had the creeps now and then; who hasn't?' Starkey's eyes lowered miserably to his hot chocolate. 'But it's nothing we can't handle. We do know you, Lil Potkin, so if you were to tell us that the reason we're feeling a bit spooky right now is that there is a ghost sitting here in the booth with us and it –'

'He,' Lil corrected her.

'If *he* is a friend of yours and he's in trouble –' Yoshi looked at Velma for approval and she nodded – 'that's good enough for us. What do you need?'

'OK,' said Abe. 'Thank you.'

'Lil,' said Nedly. 'Would you – you know.' He nodded towards Yoshi and Velma.

'Right. Abe could you do some introductions?' Lil smiled encouragingly.

Abe cleared his throat. 'Yoshi, Velma.' He opened his hand towards them and then used his rubber fingers to point at the empty seat beside Lil. 'This is . . .' He nodded. 'You know, The One.'

'Nedly,' said Lil.

'Yep,' said Abe.

Starkey said, 'He's a spectral manifestation.'

Lil said, 'He's a kid, like me. He likes comics and animals and he helps Abe out with investigations.'

Minnie gave her gum a determined chew. 'Nedly's the name of the ghost, right?'

'Right,' Lil and Abe said at the same time.

There was a pause. Nedly whispered, 'Everyone is staring at me.'

Lil looked round the table. Except for Abe, each eye was fixed on the corner where Nedly sat. 'It's no use,' she told them, 'you can't see him no matter how hard you look.'

'I was wondering,' said Yoshi shyly, pushing the condiments towards Lil, 'could Nedly move the pepper pot to the left? Just so we know he's really here.'

Lil sighed. A pulse of light travelled to the tip of Nedly's finger and the pepper pot slid to the left and fell over. Everyone shivered.

Velma chipped in, 'Could Nedly lift it into the air? Hover it?'

The pepper pot flipped up and then continued, into the air until it was wobbling about at shoulder height. They gasped. Nedly was grinning so hard he was practically glowing. Lil realised with a twinge that this might be what he had always wanted, even more than being safe. He wanted to be seen, just like everyone else.

Minnie said, 'Can Nedly –'

Lil snatched the pepper pot out of the air. 'Nedly can do all sorts of incredible things – he's literally the most amazing person I've ever met.' Nedly's face blushed brightly, and the tips of Lil's ears reddened. 'But if we don't stop Ghostcatcher, he won't be doing any of them, so let's focus on how we do that and we can come back to the tricks later, OK?'

Everyone looked down and murmured, '*OK*.'

'Good,' said Lil. 'So, what we need now is to simulate a haunting, here at the Nite Jar.' She turned to Starkey. 'Can we create a sort of electromagnetic charge that EGON would register as a ghost?'

He rolled his eyes up to think about it. 'That wouldn't be problematic but we can't suppress the one that Nedly himself makes, and there would be no guarantee they would follow the decoy.'

'How about if Nedly starts haunting here, enough to alert EGON and lure Ghostcatcher into the city,' suggested Minnie. 'Then, as soon as they are near enough to pick up the reading on their handheld devices, we switch to the decoy.'

'I could be the decoy!' offered Starkey.

'Do you have a car?' asked Velma.

Starkey face fell. 'I could get on a bus?'

'Too risky,' said Lil. 'They could board it. How about you take the Zodiac?'

Abe choked on an apple puff. 'That's *my* car you're talking about.'

'Right,' agreed Lil. 'It might not start when we need it, then we will be in trouble. You could borrow my bike?'

'I can ride a bike,' Starkey agreed brightly. 'Can I fix a cart to it?'

'Do you have a cart?'

His face fell again.

'I have a cart,' said Minnie. 'An old one. You could use that.'

Abe put his hand on Starkey's shoulder. 'You

just need to give them the run-around long enough for us to get EGON out of the game.'

'I won't let you down,' Starkey whispered, his eyes glistening with emotion.

'How about you, Minnie?' said Lil.

'I'll keep watch. There's a phone box on Bun Hill, just before the road turns towards the asylum. That way I can signal whether they are coming or going, and Irving can contact me directly with the action from town.'

Lil nodded. 'As soon as they're clear I'll go in.'

'*I'll* go in,' corrected Abe.

'We can both go in, and find EGON,' said Lil. 'See if we can dismantle it somehow.'

Starkey shook his head. 'You can't take it apart, I told you. The only way to stop EGON would be with a supercharge of electromagnetic energy, enough to melt its circuits.' He nodded at the corner. 'The kind of surge that Nedly could generate.'

Lil and Nedly exchanged worried glances. 'If Nedly's going in, then we have to find a way to deactivate the fence. It can sense him; it won't let him pass without tripping the alarm.' She pulled a glacé cherry off a Bakewell slice, threw it up in the air and tried to catch it but it bounced off her chin.

Minnie pointed at the map with a teaspoon. 'The perimeter fence runs along here. There's the track from the main road and then this area off to the side is woodland.' Her spoon scored a line from the gate to the asylum building. 'The controls are located in an outhouse on the west side of the asylum. It should be a simple on/off switch – easy enough to operate. The gate is locked electrically so once you cut the power it should be a swizz to open it. The real challenge is going to be how you get past the fence in the first place to switch it off.'

Lil chewed on her pencil. 'Margaret made it under the fence last time. Do you think we could train her up to switch off the alarm?'

At the sound of her name Margaret jumped onto Abe's lap and sat down with her shoulders back and her chin up. It was her best alert pose: *Ready for business, you can count on me.*

Abe tucked his chin in to his collar and gave her an apologetic look. 'She can do that bit all right; she's got the smarts to find her way in. And Sit! Stay! Lie down! Fetch! None of that is a problem. Find the outhouse on the edge of the west wing of the asylum, open the door, locate the control panel for the gate and perimeter fence and then throw the switch that deactivates the alarm. I just think it's an instruction too far. Even for a smart dog.'

Margaret cocked her head to one side.

Starkey creased his brows at her. 'It's no reflection on you as a dog.'

Margaret dropped her head. Lil gave her an encouraging scratch and said: 'Now, don't let it get you down. If it could be done by a dog, then it would be you but you'd be going in cold with only a map to guide you.' Lil slid the map out from under the condiments and cups and held it in front of Margaret's face.

The little dog sniffed it, pushed her wet nose against it for long enough to leave a comet of slime there and then looked at Lil again. 'Plus,' said Lil, 'if the door has a round handle, you just don't have the thumbs.'

Minnie reached into her pocket, pulled out a cold sausage and offered it up. 'We're going to need to think of something else.' Margaret took the sausage out of Minnie's hand, then leapt back under the table to eat in private.

Abe rubbed his jaw. 'Do we know anyone else small enough to get under that fence?'

Lil looked at Nedly. 'I can think of someone.'

Chapter 16

Babyface Gets Spooked

Ever since Babyface had relayed the events of the night when Nedly had gone missing, Lil had checked in on him at the Hawks Memorial Orphanage on a regular basis to have a game of snakes and ladders or share a bag of liquorice toffees, but really the visits were as much for Nedly too. He missed his old friend.

Lil left her bike by the front path, saluted up at the little bald head that had appeared in one of the top-floor windows and got a wave back.

'Look,' said Nedly, pointing to a large bare patch of land at the side of the orphanage. Where the allotment had been there were just a few grey slimy stalks lying flat across the soil.

The orphanage caretaker, Mr Kolchak, was forking over the land, pulling at the decaying plants and then dropping them into a fire he had going in an old oil drum. He paused, leaning on the fork as though it was a crutch. Lil approached softly and laid a hand his arm.

Mr Kolchak's wild eyebrows leapt up. 'Young Lilian! Excuse me, I was in another world.' He looked older than the last time Lil had seen him, which was less than a fortnight ago.

'What happened here?'

He raised his hand helplessly. 'It all just died. We had sprouts in here and leeks and the cauliflowers, not to mention the rhubarb and asparagus. And the fruit bushes. Everything.' He hung off the fork again and stared at the soil. 'Maybe it's some kind of disease. I don't know.'

Lil looked out across the field towards the

peak of Bun Hill. 'Can you dig a garden elsewhere?'

Mr Kolchak's eyelids drooped for a second and he tried to smile. Weariness hung off him like rain-soaked wool. 'I'm sure I can. Anyway, don't you worry. Get yourselves in the warm. I bet young Clark will be glad to see you!'

They crept upstairs to the third-floor landing and tiptoed to the door to Babyface's room.

'Ready?'

Nedly gulped and nodded. 'Don't expect too much from him. OK?'

Lil gave him a *when do I ever ask too much?* kind of look and then knocked.

'Lil!' The little boy beamed. His pale, finely furred head was blue-tinged with the lacework of veins below his skin, his cheeks were chapped and rosy and his button nose was orange-tipped with a brewing cold. He was wearing a brown and green turtleneck jumper and orange corduroy trousers and some baggy moccasin slippers that seemed at least two sizes too big.

Babyface took a seat at a little wooden chair

in front of a desk, opened up the lid and pulled out a sheet of card. He held it to his chest for a second and then offered it up.

It was a collage of three stick figures. One wore a yellow mac, one had a bald head and the other was taller with fair hair and a grey sweatshirt. 'It's us,' Babyface said, pointing at each figure with his little red digit. 'You, me and Ned.'

'It's really good.'

'You don't think your ears are too small in the picture?' he said, wrinkling his nose at her and then at the collage.

'No, I think you have them just right.' She ruffled his head in mock annoyance. 'You've got some fuzz growing.'

'Careful,' he said raising his hands to his crown. 'Don't rub it away. I was going to ask Mr Kolchak to put my picture on the wall, for when you're not here,' he added.

Lil pulled out a large bag of liquorice toffees and dropped them on the desk. 'Here. I brought you some supplies.'

'I'll never eat all of those,' Babyface breathed anxiously.

'Share them with your friends then.'

Babyface blinked a few times and then put his woollen hat on. He pulled a handful of toffees out of the bag and laid them on his bedspread. The misty-eyed old bear that Abe had pocketed at the doll hospital was there on his pillow. Babyface divided up the toffees carefully, half to the bear.

Nedly watched him sadly.

That afternoon it was Babyface's turn with the orphanage train set and so Lil helped him to lay out the warped old rails in a circle on the rug and they made a start on the toffees until both their mouths were black.

'I like this fast one.' Babyface gave Lil a little red tin engine to inspect and picked up a green one with a wagon on the back. 'This was Ned's best one.' He opened and closed the little doors. 'Once the older kids dropped it in the water butt but Ned fished it out with two coat hangers twisted together and when he got it, guess what?'

'There was a snail inside it!' chuckled Nedly.

'There was a snail inside it!' repeated Lil.

The little boy giggled too and then a shadow crossed his brow. 'How did you know that?'

Lil flicked a glance at Nedly. He shrugged back. Lil threw an unwrapped toffee in the air and caught it in her mouth. It was a good a time as any. 'I know because he told me.'

Babyface narrowed his eyes at her. 'When did he tell you?'

Lil took a deep breath. 'Babyface, there's something you need to know.'

The little boy eyed her soberly, then he crossed his legs and put his hands in his lap and said, 'All right.'

'Mr Kolchak told you what happened to Ned, didn't he?'

The light in the room buzzed dimly and a draught whispered at the baggy old curtains.

'He's dead,' Babyface whispered.

Lil creased her brows and gave Nedly a small careful smile and then broadened it for Babyface.

'That's right. But sometimes, even though someone is dead, a part of them can still be around.'

Babyface put the flat of his hand against his chest, 'Here, in your heart.'

Lil nodded impatiently. 'Yes, they will always be in your heart.'

'And here,' Babyface continued, pointing a finger at his temple. 'In your memories.'

'Yes, that too, but sometimes, in very special cases, a real part of them can actually exist even after they have gone.'

'A skeleton!' Babyface gasped.

Lil took a big gulp of air and tried to keep her voice as casual and reasonable-sounding as she could. 'Not a skeleton, a ghost.'

Babyface's small red cheeks drained of colour. 'I'm scared of ghosts.'

'Yeah,' said Lil. 'Most of the time I am too, but you wouldn't be scared of Ned Stubbs's ghost, would you? He wouldn't be scary.' Babyface shivered and then Lil shivered. 'And even if he was, it wouldn't be on purpose.'

'I still think I'd be frightened.'

'No, you wouldn't be.'

Babyface stuck out his lip. 'I would.'

'No, you wouldn't.' Lil rolled her eyes, 'Are you frightened now? Because he's right here in this room.'

'AAAAHHHHH!' Babyface howled.

'Great,' said Nedly.

'Button it, Babyface,' Lil hissed at him. 'It's not that scary and you know it.' He glared at her through tear-beaded eyelids and then opened his mouth to howl again. 'He's still your friend, isn't he? Even though he's dead.' Lil looked at Nedly for help.

'Go easy on him, Lil,' he whispered. 'It's a lot to take in and he's only small.'

'Take it back,' Babyface whimpered.

Lil shook her head gently and kept quiet for a moment to give the news a chance to soak in, and then she said, 'He's only changed a little bit. Otherwise, he's the same person, your good pal Ned. Wouldn't you want to hang out again, like old times?'

'Hang out with a ghost?' Babyface looked horrified.

'Give it a try?' Lil said softly. 'He's right there, in the corner.'

Babyface blinked at her, and his terrified gaze slid over to where she was pointing.

'We came here to ask you a favour. We need your help with something, Babyface. Ned does.'

Eventually the little boy gave her a small nod and Lil licked the end of an old dried-up felt-tip and drew him a diagram on the back of the collage to help explain the plan. When she had finished Babyface gave her a scandalised look.

'One, we're not supposed to go near the asylum now, especially after what happened to Ned. Two, I would have to go out after it's dark, which is also against the rules. Three, I don't think I would be allowed to . . . to . . .'

'Disable the alarm system,' Lil filled in helpfully.

'Not that either.'

'You wouldn't be on your own.'

'Is Ned coming?'

Lil shook her head. 'He has to be at the Nite Jar, luring Ghostcatcher.' Babyface's expression drooped. 'But even better –' Nedly tried to stop her from talking but she batted him away and continued – 'there's a dog, a small one – her name is Margaret.'

Babyface's lips curled downwards. 'I'm scared of dogs.'

Lil couldn't help rolling her eyes again. 'Not this one you won't be. This one is a whole lot less scary than that mangy old bear thing on your bed.'

'Tuft.' Babyface corrected her. 'Mr Mandrel gave it to me. It looked after him when he was small like I am.'

Lil flicked a glance at Nedly. *What a yarn.* 'You haven't even met her yet so how do you know?'

'I just know.'

'Five minutes ago you said you were scared of ghosts too. Just give Margaret a go, all right? She's a good dog. I know you'll like her.'

Lil sat on her hands. She Squinted at the

little boy for as long as she could while his head sank further and further into the collar of his turtleneck until his nose was just poking out of the rim.

'If there was someone else we could ask . . .'

Babyface's nose stopped the rest of his head following his chin. He peered out of the jumper like he wanted it to swallow him.

'Lil,' Nedly whispered. 'It doesn't matter; we'll find another way. He doesn't have to do it, not if it scares him.'

Lil's patience was running low. 'The plan won't work without him so, yes,' she insisted, 'he does have to do it, even if it scares him. '

Babyface was listening, his eyes on the corner where Nedly was standing and then back to Lil. 'Is that what Ned said, that I didn't have to do it if it frightened me?' He stuck his bottom lip out and it trembled a bit.

Lil shook her head at Nedly but Babyface's eyes were drawn back to the corner.

'That's exactly what Ned would have said.' A wave of goose pimples rose over the little boy's cheek and he shivered. 'Is he sometimes here, even when you're not?' he asked Lil.

Lil checked Nedly's face for the answer. 'We mostly hang around together, but he might look in every now and again – just to check that you're OK.'

Babyface nodded solemnly. 'I get the creeps sometimes, I just wondered if that was him.'

'Everyone gets the creeps sometimes,' said Lil.

Babyface nodded again. He flipped over the paper to the collage side, swivelled it towards the corner so that Nedly could see it and smiled shyly.

Lil raised her eyebrows. 'So will you help?'

Babyface looked back down at the three figures and touched the grey one with his finger.

'I'll try.'

Chapter 17

Under the Wire

As darkness fell, the Zodiac limped out of Peligan City. Its dirty, butter-coloured headlights traced the road that wound to the west as it staggered up Bun Hill carrying Abe, Lil, Margaret and Minnie towards the old asylum. They pulled over when they reached the phone box and Minnie held out her hand. 'Better give me the torch.'

Lil pursed her lips. 'You don't have one?'

'What do I need a torch for? I'm a hot dog

seller.' Lil and Abe both kept their eyes on the windscreen. 'Well . . . come on, one of you must have one. I can't do the signal without it.'

Lil folded. Reluctantly she reached into her pocket. 'You can have mine.'

Minnie nodded, turned it on and then off to test it. 'Watch for my sign. One flash when Nedly's doing his stuff at the Nite Jar; two flashes when Ghostcatcher are on their way there.'

'OK,' said Lil, watching her torch disappear inside one of Minnie's jackets. 'Once we're in the facility use the Haunting Hotline if you need to send a warning. I think it must ring there.'

Ten minutes later, Lil, Abe and Margaret were standing in the shelter of a thicket of gnarled blackthorns a few feet back from the perimeter fence. The gate to Rorschach joined the railings to the left of them. The burnt-brick shell of the ruined asylum leered at them from the horizon; its glassless windows were empty eye sockets, its doorway was a mouth with knocked-in teeth. Behind it the pale glow of the research facility shone, a second moon rising.

Abe's binoculars were trained on the hillside, waiting for the signal.

Lil glanced at her watch and then looked back into the blackness behind them, to where the orphanage lights were just twinkling on the hill, like an island in the middle of a deep and dangerous sea. 'He's not going to show,' she said. 'I should never have asked him; he's just a little kid.' She pulled her eyes away and used them to measure the gap under the fence. 'I'll do it.'

Abe flicked a sideways glance at her. 'You won't fit.'

'I'll dig it out a bit underneath, make the hole bigger.'

'What with? The signal is going to come at any minute.'

Lil pulled out a pencil and chewed on it. 'Maybe if you drive back to the phone box, tell Minnie to call the Nite Jar and warn them we'll need longer, then block the road once they've passed in case they turn back, that will give me time to dig.'

Abe held his pincer up. 'I'm not leaving you here to dig the tunnel on your own. I don't even think we should dig a tunnel.'

'It's not a tunnel; it's just a dip in the ground.'

'It's too risky.'

Lil lowered her voice. 'Nedly is counting on me. I won't let him down.'

'Neither will I,' a small voice cut through the darkness.

There was a crackle of twigs, Margaret struck her alert pose, and Babyface Kennedy climbed through the tangle of old branches to join them, the moonlight glancing off his hairless head. He was wearing a navy blue cagoule and his small fingers clutching the straps of his rucksack reminded Lil of Waldo's paws.

'You came.' Lil grinned at him, even though a sudden misgiving uncurled itself in her belly. He looked smaller there in the wilderness.

'Is Ned here?' Babyface asked hopefully.

'No, he's at the Nite Jar Cafe in town – he's doing the decoy, remember?' Babyface bit his lip. He looked back at the orphanage and then at the asylum and shivered. 'This is Margaret. She's going with you.'

Babyface cautiously approached Margaret. She sat down and looked up at him. 'Margaret, this is Babyface.'

'It's Clark, actually,' he reminded her. 'But you can call me Babyface. Everyone does . . .'

Lil bobbed down to address them both eye to eye. 'Babyface, Margaret is the smallest so you need to look after her, OK?'

'Me?'

'Think you can handle it?'

Babyface gulped. Then he took a deep breath and nodded.

Abe took Margaret's lead from his pocket and clipped it onto her collar. He held the looped end out for Babyface to take hold of, saying, 'Stick together.' Babyface gave Margaret an apprehensive look. Margaret sat down and lifted her chin nobly, like a little general, appearing dependable but not fierce.

'Do you remember where you're going?' Lil asked him. Babyface's hand trembled as he pointed a cold-reddened finger through the railings.

'Have you got the instructions?'

He reached into his pocket, pulled out a neatly folded sheet of lined paper and passed it over. Lil opened it up to the moonlight to check they had covered all eventualities.

'When you get to it there will be a lever; you just need to pull it down. If there's more than one lever, just pull them all down.' She looked him over. 'You'll be pretty well camouflaged in those dark clothes but your face is going to shine like a nightlight out there.'

Babyface knelt down on the soggy grass verge, sank his hands into the mud and then rubbed a stripe across his forehead, down his nose and under each eye.

He held his muddy hands out grimacing. Abe sighed, pulled out his crumpled handkerchief and wiped them clean. 'Pretty good,' said Lil. Babyface's bald dome still shone over his dirty face like a winter sunrise, so she pulled up his hood.

'I'm ready.' Babyface took a deep steadying breath, turned to the railings and held out his hand to take hold of Margaret's lead.

Lil eyed him critically. 'Do you really need the rucksack?'

'It's got Tuft in it.'

Abe chuckled awkwardly. 'It's just that you're a bit bulky at the moment, kid. How about you leave the teddy here, under the trees?'

Babyface shook his head stubbornly. 'No way. Tuft is coming with me.' He narrowed his eyes at Abe. 'You said Tuft would look out for me after Wool disappeared.'

'I did,' Abe said through gritted teeth. 'But he can look out for you from here, long distance.'

Babyface stuck out his bottom lip. Abe looked helplessly at Lil.

'All right,' said Lil. 'But it's going to be tight.'

They all stood watching the pitch blackness under the line of the hill. After a couple of minutes Margaret pricked up her ears. Out on the hill the torchlight blinked.

'OK,' said Lil. 'Nedly is in place and haunting.'

They waited a few minutes more, breathing softly and listening to the sound of the rain dripping. Two headlights appeared in the drive, as the Ghostcatcher van swung round the asylum towards them, twin beams like arms reaching towards the city. The van kicked up mud and water as it sped down the drive, barely slowing at the gates for them to open ahead of it and then raced through and away up the lane. Abe, Lil and Babyface watched the back lights fade and then go out completely as it turned a bend. As one their eyes went to the summit where Minnie stood. Blink-blink – the second signal.

Abe poked a thumb in the direction of the asylum. 'Time to go.'

Babyface gave a solemn nod and hoisted the

bag up securely. The metal railing cast a striped pattern of shadows over his round face.

Abe patted him strongly on the back. 'We'll be right behind you, kid.'

Babyface turned to Margaret. 'Don't worry. I'll look after you.' And then he laid himself as flat as possible beside the fence to roll under it. Lil had to knead the rucksack past the railings and push him through like a roll of dough. He arrived on the other side coated with wet earth. Margaret shimmied under after him.

Lil stood close by the fence. 'Once you've sorted the alarm, you and Margaret come straight back here and find Minnie at the phone box. Stay with her until we find you, OK?'

Babyface's eyes darted between the deserted lane that led back to the orphanage and the ruined building ahead. 'Just don't be too long.'

'No fear.' Lil tried out a smile. 'We'll be in and out before you know it.'

He crossed his fingers on both hands and held them up for Lil to see, then turned away and stumbled off into the wilderness with Margaret bounding alongside him. His hood fell down as he ran. As they reached the flower beds that were now filled with weeds, clouds drew across the moon like a curtain and the garden grew dark.

Just once Lil caught sight of the pale orb of his head bobbing along the path and then it was swallowed up in the shadows of the old asylum.

Abe and Lil stared out across the straggly lawn and then up at the gate, then back across the lawn.

'What was that?' Abe rushed his binoculars to his eyes one-handed. He stretched out his middle finger and inched the focus wheel. 'I thought I saw something.'

'Babyface?'

'No, it was a light.

'Maybe a fox?'

'With a torch?' He gave her a look and then went back to his binoculars, straining his eyes against the darkness.

'Let's have a go.' Lil reached up for them and Abe gave a strangled yelp. 'Sorry, I didn't know you had tied them round your neck.' She held her hand out. 'Can I have the binoculars?'

Abe shook his head stubbornly. 'If there's any looking to do, I'll do it.' He peered through them again. 'Maybe it was a trick of the moon.'

They moved closer to the railings. The rain was the fine sort that floated innocently in the air and soaked things. They watched the empty lawn in silence, their faces lit red by the bulbs over the gate.

Abe muttered to himself and shook his head.

'What did you say?' said Lil.

'I said why don't you let me take care of it? I can bust EGON's head by myself.'

'No, you can't; only Nedly can take him out of the game completely and I need to be there with him so – Abe!' She gasped suddenly. His face had turned green. The lights had changed.

There was a clunking sound and the gate

lost power. 'They did it!' Lil almost laughed with relief.

Tentatively Abe took hold of the wet metal bars of the gate and pushed.

'We're in.'

Chapter 18

Rorschach Research Facility

The gate swung open so quickly that Abe had to chase it to stop it clanging against the railings. He waited while Lil crossed the threshold, then gently closed it behind them.

'With any luck we'll be out again before they get back but if not . . . hopefully they'll assume it's a malfunction – the wiring in the asylum can't be up to much these days.' He paused for a moment to give Lil a concerned eyeball. 'Ready?'

'Ready,' she confirmed.

Abe looked grimly out at the asylum and flexed his multi-purpose pliers. 'All right, let's go.'

They crouch-ran from the lane and then across the long straggly lawn, the grass heavy with dew-like raindrops. Midway they linked up with the trampled route that Babyface and Margaret had taken. A soft bark sounded and the small figures of a boy and a dog emerged from the shadow of the asylum and began running towards them. Babyface looked exhilarated, his cheeks were red beneath the mud and his eyes shone.

'We did it!' he gasped.

'Good work, kid,' Abe said sternly, with one eye on the landscape.

Babyface gulped breathlessly. 'The door was open and the light was on so we knew straight away where it was. And there was a card stuck over the levers that said which ones deactivated things!'

Abe and Lil exchanged glances. 'Too easy.'

Babyface frowned. 'It was quite hard actually. It was dark and haunted and the grass was long and wet and difficult.' He looked at Margaret for support. 'If I hadn't had Tuft with me for luck . . .'

'Yeah,' Lil said quickly. 'You were really brave and you did it.' She gave him a high-five.

The breeze picked up and rippled the surface of the grass. Abe gave the white haze that was shining around the asylum a foreboding look. 'I don't like this.'

'Me neither.' Lil zipped up her mac. 'But this is our only shot so we better take it.'

He turned to her. 'Look, I can handle it from here. You take Babyface and head back.'

'No way –' Lil began.

'It could be a trap.'

Lil gave him the Squint. 'You take Babyface back if you're so worried. I'll find and destroy EGON with Nedly. I told you before: we can manage on our own.'

'And I told you before: there's no way I'm leaving you to do this alone.'

'I won't be alone. Nedly will be here in a minute.'

Abe gave her a look. 'We don't have time to stand around here arguing about it.'

Lil opened her mouth, closed it again and then said, 'Agreed. Babyface, you and Margaret go and find Minnie in the phone box. Any trouble, call the number.'

'What number?'

'The Haunting Hotline – Minnie knows.'

Lil pulled Babyface's hood back up and hoisted his rucksack firmly onto his shoulders. 'It's a long way up the hill so be careful in the dark, and stay off the road.'

'Margaret, sit,' Abe instructed her. Margaret sat down and cocked her head, ready for action. 'Find Minnie.'

Babyface tightened his grip on the lead.

'If anything happens, stick with the dog,' Lil told him. 'She'll get you home safely.'

The door to the outhouse in the west wing was wide open and lit up, just as Babyface had described it. Someone had left a paraffin lamp burning on the side and the warm yellow glow was almost inviting, but the outhouse didn't look like it was used very much. Dead beetles and crumpled spiders littered the floor, rusty spades and garden forks were cobwebbed against the wall. *So why was the lamp there?*

'Might as well have put out a welcome mat,' Abe growled.

They skirted the west wing of the ruins, following the white orb of light that stretched into the night. Past the ivy and thick stems of thorny rose bushes that were pulling at the asylum bricks, circling out like coils of razor wire. Lil cast a quick look over her shoulder. The gate was a long way off but it was still lit green and unlocked.

The wind picked up, throwing rain in their faces. Lil shivered suddenly as a wave of dread washed over her. A sharp crackle split the air, and with a faint burning smell Nedly appeared mid-run, staggering forward as he tried to slow himself down.

'Nedly?' Abe asked the damp, black night.

'He's here.' Lil breathed out her relief.

'Phew!' said Nedly as he came to a stop with the air of someone who had just broken the ribbon at the finishing line. He bent over for a minute with his hands on his hips and then circled back round to where they were standing. 'I made it!'

He grinned at Lil and Abe, then a shadow passed over his face as he looked up at the asylum looming above, dark and fractured by fire and he turned as grey as a moonlit cloud.

Lil tried to snap him out of it, with a quick, 'Hey! Everything go to plan?' Nedly nodded distractedly. She made an 'OK' sign and held it up to Abe.

Nedly shivered and looked about him. 'Babyface made it then?'

Lil kept her eyes on the murky woodland that hemmed the asylum grounds and tried to smile bravely. 'So far, so good, but we have no time to waste. Ghostcatcher will catch up with Starkey eventually and when they do they will come right back here. We need to be long gone by then.'

'Agreed,' said Abe and Nedly at the same time.

'Here's how we'll play it,' Abe continued. 'You two wait back there in the outhouse, stay out of sight. I'm going to check out the facility. There might be a caretaker or security guard lurking around, so keep Nedly out of the way until I find EGON and confirm that the coast is clear.'

Lil opened her mouth to argue but Abe cut in. 'It's Nedly they're after,' he warned her. 'If anyone comes – make a run for it. Don't wait for me. Promise?'

Lil didn't promise but she said, 'Be careful.'

'Don't worry about me. I've been casing joints for years.' They watched Abe crouch-run towards the cold light of the Research Facility and heard a gasp and a flump as he stumbled over one of the old flower beds.

They stood just inside the outhouse, sheltered from the rain, waiting. After a minute Lil said,

'I feel like we're on stage with this light on us,' and turned off the lamp. They let their eyes adjust to the gloom.

A fox cried out in the woods. Lil took out a pencil and started chewing it. Her breath plumed out like steam, joining the mist in the air, and she shrugged her mac closer. Nedly was sending out a powerful case of the creeps. 'So,' she said conversationally. 'How did it go down at the Nite Jar? Give me the details.'

'It was good,' Nedly started. 'Starkey was great; his field-generating thing looked like a big speaker hooked up to a car battery. He strapped it onto the cart with some old rope and then pitched it so it gave off a signal a bit like mine. Yoshi and Velma kept watch and as soon as Ghostcatcher arrived Starkey sprang to action. Once they were fully out of the van and had their EMF readers going I had to keep really still while Starkey turned up his generator full blast. Once they had both locked on to him Velma gave the signal and he jumped onto your bike and started up the road. As soon as they started to follow I got out of there and came and found you.' He gave her an encouraging smile. 'Like clockwork.'

'It was a crack team, just like Abe promised.' Lil grinned back. 'What did you do for the haunting part?'

'A combination of moves I'd been working on. I shifted some things around on the tables as a warm-up, then I kicked a copy of the *Herald* and all the pages fell apart and went over the floor. Then I floated a ketchup bottle through the air,' he added nonchalantly.

Lil raised her eyebrows. 'Impressive.'

'Twice round the room. I kept away from the china and glass so I didn't break anything if I dropped it. So I just used mustard bottles, serviettes, forks . . .'

The fox cried again – at least, they hoped it was fox; it sounded lower than before.

'. . . and tea towels,' he continued shakily.

Lil looked out into the darkness. The wet night carried the smell of old soot, and the presence of the asylum seemed huge, like a brick tsunami that had risen silently and hung frozen right behind them. Lil could feel it, but she couldn't bring herself to look in case that broke the spell and brought the whole thing crashing down.

Her leg started jigging nervously. 'What's keeping Abe so long?' She flicked a glance at Nedly. His eyes had grown larger or his face had shrunk; either way his face was pinched-looking and his skin shone palely, like a pearl underwater. 'There were three of them there, though, right?'

'What?' he whispered.

'At the Nite Jar.' Nedly frowned back at her, not understanding. 'Because you said that they *both* locked on to Starkey's generator. That's two.'

He thought for a moment. 'Maybe the third one was behind them? I didn't stick around.'

'Right,' said Lil, accidently chewing an inch of wood off the end of her pencil. She rolled it around a few times and then spat it into the grass. Her heart was thumping out a warning.

'I think I should go and look for Abe. Otherwise we're going to run out of time. You stay here.'

'No way, what if you don't come back either? I'm not staying here on my own.' He shot a glance that was full of dread at the wall behind him. 'Not here.'

'No.' Lil understood. 'OK, we'll go together.'

No sooner had Lil's shoe leather hit the grass than a phone started ringing. The sound cut through the eerie night like an alarm bell. She and Nedly looked at each other. 'Is that the Haunting Hotline? Do you . . . do you think someone is calling in a tip? Or is it Minnie, phoning to warn us that Ghostcatcher are heading back?'

Nedly shrugged anxiously. Lil's heart was racing now. The phone trilled out again. We should try to find it,' she whispered. 'See who it is.'

Neither moved. The phone rang a third time. And then it stopped.

Chapter 19

EGON

The sudden silence that followed felt even more alarming than the sound of the phone ringing in the deserted grounds. Lil shot back into the shadows and gulped. 'It didn't ring for very long.'

Nedly peered down the length of the west wing. 'Did someone answer it?'

'Abe must have,' Lil said confidently, and then faltered. 'But if that was Minnie on the Haunting Hotline –'

'– it means Ghostcatcher are on their way back.'

'And the decoy didn't work.' Lil stuck the pencil in her mouth and bit down on it hard. 'And we're almost out of time. Come on!'

She started to run, skimming along beside the asylum wall. Nedly caught up with her at the corner, and as they rounded the side of the building the research facility came into view.

Powerful floodlights encircled a colony of white domed tents, like giant glowing jellyfish, their surfaces billowing in the breeze. Thick cables snaked across the grass and into the tents and the background hum of a generator drowned out the patter of raindrops.

Lil searched the scene for any signs of disturbance. 'Where is Abe?'

She looked back to the darkness that held the lawn, the fence and the woods behind them. She couldn't even make out the hill with the phone box.

'We should find him and go,' said Nedly, looking jumpy.

'Not until we've done what we came here for,' said Lil as a feeling of dread started to grow in the pit of her stomach. 'Quit giving me the creeps, Nedly; I'm trying to concentrate.'

'Sorry,' he said miserably. 'I just don't like it here.'

'I know,' Lil replied. 'So the sooner we take care of business and get out the better, right?'

'Right,' said Nedly, steeling himself for action. 'I'll go first.'

'Wait!' said Lil. 'Not this time. If EGON is watching, then you might not be invisible. I'll go first.'

The rain appeared white in the floodlights, a haze of water droplets falling through the dark around the tents. Lil stepped out towards them and then stopped. She could hear a strange pulsing sound like an electrical swell coming from the asylum and turned to locate it.

The white glare struck the wall with the severity of lightning, creating shadows between the crumbling bricks and behind the broken glass of the windows. At the bottom of the wall was a set of tilted wooden trapdoors – an old coal bunker. A thick red cable was pinched between them.

Lil's shadow sharpened and shrank as she neared the building. She crouched before the bunker and the throbbing grew louder. 'There's something here!' She took hold of one of the iron ring handles and felt the cold metal vibrating in her hands.

The trapdoor opened with a creak. Lil leant over, peering into the cave-like room.

'What is it?' Nedly appeared suddenly behind her.

Lil gasped, and let the door fall with a bang that echoed loudly.

'Sorry,' he winced.

Lil took a deep breath, opened the trapdoor again and this time, with Nedly standing guard, she took a couple of steps down into the bunker.

Inside was like a blue-lit grotto, cold, damp and smelling of fumes. A large cylindrical battery the size of a small car was suspended in the centre of the room between two huge brackets. Electric currents whiplashed across its surface and its sides were plastered with biohazard signs and warnings. Piles of shining black stones were heaped against each wall, glistening in the cold light.

'It's the tourmaline,' whispered Nedly.

Lil looked at the stones and then at a thick red pipeline that was connected to the front of the battery.

'They're powering EGON with this stuff, aren't they?' Her eyes gleamed electric blue. 'So if we follow the pipeline, it should lead us right to its door.'

'Do you think Abe discovered all this too?' said Nedly.

'Probably,' said Lil.

They followed the red cable on its path through the tents, stepping over wooden walkways that connected like extremely low bridges and hopscotching the smaller wires that hid in the grass, until she saw it disappear into a bell-shaped tent in the middle of the colony. 'Pssst, Nedly,' she whispered. 'I think this is it.'

Lil flattened herself against the tent's silk-thin walls. 'Abe?' she whispered.

No answer.

'Abe?' she tried again, more loudly this time

She stuck her head quickly through the tent flap. In the soft white sheen of the floodlights diffused by the tent material she saw immediately that Abe wasn't there, but EGON was.

It was the size of a garden shed. A rectangle of brushed steel with rounded corners. Its surface was almost completely smooth except for at the centre where there was a dull black screen and beneath it a keyboard. A panel of dials and a single metal switch were on one side of the screen.

An empty operator chair on wheels was in front of the control panel. To the left was a card table, three folding chairs and a camp bed.

Nedly crept in behind her and they both stood staring.

'Abe isn't here.' Nedly bit his lip.

'He's probably got lost, that's all. I bet he'll be here any minute,' Lil lied, trying to keep her

273

own panic in check. 'So let's get on with it, all right?' She rolled up her sleeves. 'What do we have to do?'

Nedly shrugged. 'Starkey said that I could put a reverse surge of electromagnetic energy through EGON and melt its circuits.'

'Right,' said Lil, nodding. 'Where do you think they are?'

'Somewhere inside?' Nedly eyed the large metal box apprehensively.

Lil gave it the Squint. 'Only one way to find out.'

'No way am I getting in there. What if EGON traps me?' He shook his head. 'What if I get in there but I can't get out again?'

'Good point,' Lil agreed. 'Stay out here, put your hands on the shell and melt them from the outside in.'

Nedly wriggled his shoulders and shook out his arms and at the end of his sweatshirt his hands started glowing. His fingertips turned orange, like he was shining a torch behind them, then they grew brighter, until they looked white hot. He rubbed them together briskly in a ready-for-business kind of way and then he flattened his palms and laid them squarely on EGON.

His body began trembling, his face fixed with concentration, his hair swaying in the spectral wind he was generating.

Lil watched him, fingers crossed, whispering 'Come on!' under her breath.

A few minutes later Nedly gasped, 'Is it working?'

'I can't tell,' she confessed. 'It's just blank.'

Nedly redoubled his efforts.

Lil paced back and forth a few times, blowing out her cheeks, and then, after Nedly glared at her, perched restlessly on one of the fold-up chairs. There was a book on the card table, a thick hardback with a bookmark stuck halfway in. There was something familiar about the book; it was lying face down but there was a photograph on the back cover of a man in a white lab coat, a man with deep-set eyes. Lil stared at it for a moment. 'Can you feel its insides melting now?' she asked distractedly.

Nedly grimaced and tried to shake the question out of his head. 'One, I don't want to think about melted insides. And two, I keep telling you: I can't feel anything. Nothing is happening.'

He closed his eyes and bared his teeth with the prolonged effort. Lil crooked her elbow over her eyes to keep the spectral wind out of her face. 'Come on,' she said. 'You can do it; I know you can.'

After a few more minutes Nedly disengaged and slumped, exhausted, onto his knees, drooping forward until his forehead touched the floor. 'I can't do it,' he moaned.

There was a single switch on the panel, a small metal one. Lil flicked it on and off, on and off. Nothing happened. 'I don't know,' she said, flicking buttons and turning dials. 'It's like EGON is already dead.'

Nedly collapsed onto his side and laid there recovering, with his eyes closed. 'Maybe Abe did get to him first. Maybe we passed each other without noticing?'

'Maybe,' said Lil. 'But how would Abe have taken EGON out without leaving a mark on it?' She frisked EGON's surface, looking for hidden buttons, switches or weaknesses, and found a thin circle cut into the metal on its side. 'Wait, Nedly, I've got something!'

Lil scrabbled frantically at the impossibly narrow gap round the circle, trying to get a grip with her fingertips. She gave up and stuck a pencil in and broke the nib off. 'Arrrggh!' She kicked EGONs shell. 'If only Abe was here, he could jemmy this with his Swiss Army hand – wait!' she gasped. 'I have a Swiss Army knife too.' She started rummaging in her bag, unloading everything onto the floor. 'Where is it?'

Nedly opened his eyes. From his position on the floor things looked different. There, just a few feet away from where he lay was the thing they had missed. 'Lil!' he called out. 'I think I've worked out what the problem is.'

'What?' Lil looked up from her pile of stuff. Nedly got back to his feet and Lil joined him. 'The red pipeline. It's the power source.' He pointed at the cable, lying slack on the floor. 'That's why we couldn't switch him on. It's not plugged in, see? We just have to –'

They heard a sound, the snap of someone standing on a twig. Lil turned to see a shadow moving along the side of the tent. It wasn't Abe. The shadow had wavy hair and was carrying something in front of it. Lil froze, then whispered, 'Hide!'

'No need.' Lazlo Yossarian entered the tent behind the tray he was carrying, which was heavy with a cosied teapot and some cups. He was wearing a collarless shirt with an orange-silk cravat, baggy trousers, espadrilles and a large woollen cardigan. Instead of a belt a paisley sash was wrapped tightly round his waist.

He grinned broadly. 'You don't need to be afraid of me.'

Lil got to her feet, forced her eyes not to look at Nedly and said nothing.

'Have you come from the orphanage?'

He hadn't recognised her. Cautiously Lil reached for the suggestion. 'That's right,' she said slowly. 'I came from the orphanage and I got lost, then I saw the lights so I came here.'

Yossarian smiled. 'You must have come through the perimeter fence. Someone deactivated the security system, I think – it's not working anyway.

'I bet you've been wondering what we're up to out here. It's OK, I understand; kids are curious, always sneaking around. I was the same when I was small, always asking questions. That's why I became a scientist.'

Lil noticed there were three cups on the tray.

Yossarian saw her looking and smiled. 'Oh, don't worry it's just me here – the others have been called out.' He paused. 'On a mission. But I knew I had company, so I made some tea. Enough for all three of us.'

Chapter 20

Tea for Three

Lil's eyes shot around the tent before she could stop them. *Abe was here too.* She looked back at the tent flap but no one else stepped through it.

'Don't be alarmed.' Yossarian gave her a shy smile. 'Welcome, both of you!'

'Who are you talking about? There's just you and me here.' Lil held out her arms to emphasise the emptiness of the space around her.

Yossarian smiled warmly. 'We both know that's not true.'

Lil grabbed hold of her rucksack and started shoving her scattered belongings back inside it.

'Please don't go, not yet,' Yossarian said. 'I just want to talk to you, for a few minutes and then if you still want to leave, I'll help you. Agreed?'

'All right.' Lil turned to place her bag back on the floor, taking the opportunity to flick her gaze over to Nedly once and then at the flap in a way that meant, *I'll distract him, you split* and then she said: 'What do you want to talk about?'

'I want to tell you a story, something I've pieced together from notebooks and public records, newspaper articles and the word off the street.' Yossarian grinned. 'I think you'll find it interesting and at the end of it I'd like you to tell me if my story is true.'

Lil shrugged and kept her gaze low, while Nedly began to slink carefully through the tent material.

Yossarian shivered. 'It's another cold night.' He pointed at the fold-up chair. Why don't you have a seat over there away from the draught?'

'I'm all right standing.'

'It's a long story; you might feel more comfortable if you take the weight off.'

Nedly hesitated half in and half out of the tent.

Lil circled round to the table, glaring at him as she passed with a look that said, *Why are you still here*? She turned a chair so that she had a view of the door for when Abe came through it and then sat down and gave Yossarian the Cryptic Eyebrow.

'OK,' he began. 'During the "investigation" –' he crooked two fingers round the word investigation and grinned – 'into the second fire here at Rorschach, Gordian's Police Department turned up a whole archive of notebooks stashed away in the cellar, charting the genesis of Cornelius Gallows' later work on disembodiment. His notes were written in teeny-tiny handwriting on narrow lines, pages and pages of it, a decade of research all swollen with damp.

'I was the first person they called to decipher it. Many years ago I had studied Gallows' book.' He pointed to the hardback that lay on the stool. 'I wrote a paper on it, so I knew the theory, just not how to apply it.'

Yossarian poured out the tea. It smelt spicy and sweet. Lil tried to subtly nod Nedly out of the tent while he grimaced back at her insisting, 'I can't just leave you here.' When Yossarian looked up she tried to turn the nod into a thoughtful-looking agreement with whatever it was he had been saying.

'We all have our favourite books.' He smiled brightly and nodded at Lil's copy of *McNair and the Free Press*, which was still lying on the floor where she had dropped it. 'Books that change how we see the world, and remind us of its possibilities.'

Lil quickly bent down, scooped her book off the floor and shoved it into her mac pocket and then crossed her arms and slumped back in her chair, giving him an eye-roll for good luck.

'I know what you're thinking: Gallows was a fright – a total monster.' He shrugged and moved closer to EGON. 'But the science was good. It was revolutionary. He proved it was possible to die and yet still live. Just like your friend here.'

Nedly froze. The bottom dropped out of Lil's stomach, plunging her insides to ice. 'What?'

'Your friend. Here.' He met Lil's eye with a smile in his, held her gaze and then dropped his hand to the ground, grabbed the red cable and shoved it into its port.

'No!' yelled Lil.

'Lil?' shouted Nedly. 'What should I do?' EGON whirred into life, the buttons beside the black screen glowing dimly at first but then growing brighter.

'It's all right.' Yossarian held out a hand to quiet her. 'This is just so that we can keep an eye on my colleagues in the city, that's all.'

There was a pause and then the hum of a

fan and the buttons glowed and brightened. A map of Peligan City appeared on the black screen: thousands of tiny square buildings in blocks, black roads like rivulets of oil, and the Kowpye a grey snake winding through it.

Yossarian took his place in the wheelie chair and pressed a combination of buttons on the panel, then flipped the switch and a luminous green wand appeared on the map, like clock hands at midnight. He turned a dial and the wand began wiping through the city in a circle. They all watched it trailing a pale green tail as it pulsed round and round.

A blip appeared on the map. 'There's Ghostcatcher.' Yossarian pointed to a dot in Old Town, on the edge of the Saints. They're just kicking their heels, though; there's only one ghost in Peligan City now and he's right here.'

Lil glanced at Nedly with a question. *Where's Starkey?* She dug her fingernails into the sweaty palms of her hands. Then it appeared, the second blip.

Yossarian frowned. He typed in a few more

285

numbers. And then turned the dial with his head cocked, as though he was tuning a radio.

'Some kind of decoy?' He raised his eyebrows. Lil kept quiet. 'Oh well, whatever it is out there I expect it will keep them busy for a while at least.

'Now, where was I? Yes, so I read the research that was in the bunker and from that we were able to create our Projected Entrapment Matrix and the EMF readers. Once we had seen how Gallows' original experiment worked, it wasn't rocket science to reverse it.

'We were able to capture our first ghost at that haunting in Old Town.' Yossarian handed Lil a mug of tea with a smile. 'That's when we first met. Do you remember? I picked up a reading from you, a residual.

'Later, when we ran the analysis on the combined feeds from all our equipment we realised that there had been a second spirit there that night. We thought it was an echo but it was, in fact, the first recorded haunting of the Final Ghost.'

He set a second mug on the table, explaining, 'This one is for our friend. I know he probably can't drink it yet, but it would have been rude not to offer him one.'

Nedly shuffled closer to the table and cautiously lowered himself into the seat opposite Lil. He wrapped his hands round the mug as though he was warming them. Lil didn't look at him. She looked everywhere else but there.

The tea smelt of warm milk, cinnamon and ginger. Lil took a small sip. 'This doesn't taste like normal tea.'

'No, it isn't. It's a kind of spiced chai that I picked up on my travels. I put lots of honey in it.

'So . . .' He dragged the wheelie chair over, sat down again and slapped his hands on his thighs. 'By then, events had taken another turn; it was discovered that although Cornelius Gallows himself had been alive and working in Fellgate Prison, weaponising the ghosts of the prisoners there, he was now quite genuinely dead and no longer in need of his later research, personal diaries or experimental equipment, and, via Acting Mayor Gordian again, we got our hands on enough material for phase two. EGON.'

Yossarian slid back over to the controls. He flicked the switch by the keyboard and the picture changed to a green pulse that zigzagged its way across the screen like the reading on a heart monitor.

'After that point Marek and Virgil spent all their time working on EGON here, and I was left to my own devices to continue my research into the identity of the Final Ghost.

'We knew where Gallows was getting his material – I mean, victims.' He winced. 'They were all inmates in the Secure Wing for the Criminally Insane, but before that . . . it was me who discovered that Gallows' first weaponised ghost, Mr Glimmer, was created from his young apprentice, Leonard Owl –'

Lil interrupted. 'Gallows murdered Owl.'

There was a pile of playing cards on the table, next to the book. While Yossarian's back was turned Lil tried to flick one at Nedly to get his attention but he was too absorbed in the story and it fluttered straight through him.

'Yes,' said Yossarian soberly. 'That's right.' He turned back to face them. 'Coincidentally that same night an eleven-year-old went missing from the Hawks Memorial Orphanage across the road from the asylum.' Lil's tea went down the wrong way. Yossarian waited for her to stop coughing before adding, 'He was never seen alive again.'

Nedly was staring at Yossarian. He looked like he was holding his breath.

'Now, according to Gallows' notes, during the experimental procedure a boy burst in and attempted to free Owl before the lightning struck. Both were killed, though Gallows makes no reference to the mysterious boy after that, or to weaponising a second ghost.'

Yossarian typed something in to EGON's keyboard. Nedly craned closer and Yossarian shuddered suddenly but a small smile twitched at the corner of his mouth. He adjusted the dial again and then stared at the screen as though he saw something in the green pulse that interested him so greatly that he had to pull his eyes from it to continue the story.

'Following an anonymous tip one year later, Peligan City P.D. located a makeshift grave here in the grounds at Rorschach. A second body had been laid to rest alongside Leonard Owl. That body was identified as that of Ned Stubbs.' He spun his chair to face her. 'And that, Lil Potkin, is the ghost that haunts you.'

Lil tried to keep her face completely still. They sat there for a moment staring at each other and not blinking until Lil looked away.

'It's an honour to meet you, Ned Stubbs, at long last. I've read *so* much about you.'

Lil wouldn't let her eyes betray her; she bored them into a muddy footprint on the canvas.

Yossarian smiled. 'It's all right; I can see him myself now.' He pointed to the thin green line that was zigzagging across the screen. 'That's him – right there. It's the electromagnetic field

290

he's generating.' Then he looked at the chair opposite Lil and waved.

Lil glanced up at Nedly, and she could see that his eyes were gleaming.

'He can see me! He's practically looking right at me!' Nedly's heart looked like it was about to burst.

'And there,' Yossarian continued, referring back to the screen and pointing to a faint echo of Nedly's line that tracked beneath it, 'is you.'

'Which line is you?' Lil asked.

Yossarian laughed. He wheeled himself to the card table and poured Lil a second cup of tea.

'So,' he continued, 'I've been working on this idea of objects that the ghosts are bound to. We know that's how Gallows controlled them. We found pictures of the poppets in his notes, and traces of tiny metal bells in the furnace in the basement of the doll hospital. So my theory is that someone else destroyed the bound objects and therefore the spooks before we got there. It's the only explanation I can find.

'The objects are their weakness, you see. Their Achilles heel. And so I began my own project, to search for the object that the Final Ghost was bound to.'

'So you could destroy him.'

'No, I have never wanted that. Never.' He spun to face Lil and met her gaze with unflinching sincerity. 'I don't believe that the Final Ghost is bad. He's nothing like the others, are you, Ned?'

Nedly gulped and raised his eyebrows hopefully.

Lil tried unsuccessfully to kick him under the table to break the spell Yossarian was casting but he didn't notice. 'Why should we trust you?'

'Because I can help you.' Yossarian let his brow crease up with sympathy. 'You're just a kid – you should be having fun. Hanging out at the shops, drinking milkshakes . . .' He paused as he had obviously started running out of child-friendly material. 'Like . . . normal kids do. Not being chased all over Peligan City, trying to keep your friend out of danger.' Lil squinted at him. 'Aren't you tired of running?' he asked her.

He was right about one thing, Lil thought. She was tired, suddenly and extremely tired. She took another sip of tea.

'So, I asked myself, what could the Final Ghost be bound to, what links him to this mortal world? The answer was staring me in the face . . .'

Lil started to interrupt. 'He's not bound –'

But Yossarian cut her dead. 'All the ghosts created by Cornelius Gallows were bound – all of them – that's the difference between them and anyone else who dies and their spirit, or what have you, drifts away, or is reabsorbed into the universe or whatever you think happens. For a ghost to exist as a being, even an ethereal one, they must be anchored.'

'But –'

Yossarian held his finger up to quiet her. 'Even Ned Stubbs is bound to something . . . I'll prove it to you.'

'Lil?' whispered Nedly, as if he had finally noticed she was there. 'I have a bad feeling.'

Lil raised her eyebrow cynically at Yossarian, over the rim of her cup, took another sip of the tea and then tried to rest the cup on her knee, but she missed it. The tea sloshed over the floor.

'Whoops! Sorry!' Lil began, stumbling onto her feet. She stared at the liquid that laid there on the white canvas like a golden starfish, then her head began to spin and she let herself flump back onto the chair.

Yossarian gave her an appraising look, turned back to the machine and typed something into the keyboard. The pulse continued to zigzag and Yossarian gazed at it, his face bathed in the green light.

'Lil?' Nedly lurched to his feet and the chair he had been sitting on tipped over with the force of the movement.

Lil peered up at him blearily. There were two Nedlys standing there, both drifting apart. Lil blinked and they came back together again.

'That tea is very warming – isn't it?' Yossarian smiled at her. 'And you've had *such* a busy night. How are you feeling?'

'A bit woozy,' she replied honestly.

Yossarian smiled again without looking at her. The green light on his face was fading. 'That will be the sedative I slipped you – don't panic.'

Lil attempted to throw the cup away but her finger was stuck in the handle, so she just swiped with it and then let it hang from her impossibly heavy arm. She looked towards Yossarian, and tried to give him the Squint but her eyes crossed over.

'You mustn't be frightened. It's just a very strong dose,' she heard him say. 'It will slow your heart right down but it shouldn't stop it entirely, all being well.'

Lil blinked. She saw Nedly stumble to his knees. His skin looked mottled, with a bluish tinge and the corners of his lips had turned black. The dials and switches of EGON emerged through the grey of his sweatshirt. He held up a hand and his eyes widened as he stared through it; he was fading. Lil's eyelids shut.

'Wake up!' she yelled to herself and forced them open again.

Nedly's outline smudged and flickered – it looked as though he was being rubbed out somehow. Panic rose in her chest as she watched him merge with his surroundings and she realised that either Nedly was becoming invisible to her too, or he was actually disappearing.

She shook her head to try to clear it. The darkness around her seemed to be growing, like someone was turning out the lights one by one.

'WAKE UP!' she shouted again, but she wasn't listening to herself; she was floating on a soft feather bed, while the tent spun away beneath her.

Chapter 21

The Dead Connection

Lil felt someone give her cheek a firm pinch. She levered her eyelids up a fraction and peered through the lashes. She was still in the tent. Shadowy blobs sharpened before her until she could make out Yossarian sitting in front of EGON's screen, tapping his keyboard. He looked up, slid over on his wheelie chair and pulled Lil's eyelid up, shone a pen torch at her and then slid back to EGON again.

Lil blinked. Where was Nedly? She sat bolt

upright suddenly and whipped her head around, desperately searching the tent. Then she saw him, swimming back into focus.

'Are you OK?' she croaked. She tried to stand but her knees buckled.

Yossarian didn't take his eyes off the screen; the green light struck his face like a troll. 'Better take it slowly, give your body time to adjust. You were out cold for a minute there.'

'What did you do to me, you . . . you . . . ?' Lil's befuddled brain reached for the insult that was evading it and settled for an accusing glare. *He knew what he was: someone who pretends to be a friend and then turns out to be an enemy. What was that called, a werewolf? Something about a wolf . . .*

'LIL!' Nedly yelled to snap her out of it.

Yossarian turned away from his typing to give her a friendly smile. 'Just a little experiment. Nothing to worry about, but I needed to be sure.'

'Why, you . . .' Lil lurched to her feet again, swayed as though she was punch-drunk and nosedived the floor. She lay there face down until Yossarian yanked her up by one arm and propped her in the chair.

'Sit down, make yourself comfortable.' He gave her a quick shake. 'You too, Nedly.'

He grinned at Lil. 'That's what you said, when you were coming round. You called him Nedly. I like it. Deadly Nedly, the most powerful ghost in Peligan City.'

'I never called him that.'

'I'm just joking around,' Yossarian chuckled. 'Relax, the worst is over. I mean you no harm; I'm very pleased you're here, that's why I arranged all this. After that dear old fool Starkey bumbled upon our set-up here I took the opportunity to feed him enough info about EGON that I *knew* he would have to tell you, and then you would *have* to come in and try to sabotage it.

'I slipped the plans of the alarm system to a colleague at City Hall and he passed them to your friend the hot dog seller. You're a great team, really very cute, especially the little bald orphan and the dog. They weren't very good at deactivating the alarm system, but that's OK – I disabled it for them.

'You see, I wanted you to come. And so, here you are.' When he grinned there was a maniacal glint in his eye.

'I just needed to do one small experiment to prove a point.' He interlaced his fingers round one knee and hugged it tightly.

Lil couldn't feel the bones in her arms or legs; they just felt like pieces of rubber cut into limb shapes. She tried moving them about to get the blood flowing.

Yossarian humoured her with a cosy grin. 'My hypothesis was that all of the ghosts weaponised by Gallows' machine were bound to an object.'

'Nedly wasn't weaponised,' Lil persisted through gritted teeth. Her neck felt too weak to hold her head up so she let it drop.

'Agreed. He slipped through the net. Gallows left him to wander off in the ether, which he did for a long time, until he found something to be bound to.'

'But he didn't,' Lil interrupted.

'He did,' said Yossarian firmly. 'Except Nedly didn't choose an object; he chose a person.' He pushed Lil's head up until she was looking blearily at him. 'He chose you.'

Lil snorted. She opened her mouth to contradict him again but then looked at Nedly. Nedly looked back at her anxiously. She shook her head to free it of Yossarian's hand. 'It doesn't work like that,' she said uncertainly.

'Nedly's EMF signal –' Yossarian pointed to the green pulse on the screen – 'almost disappeared as you began to lose consciousness. He's linked to you, Lil Potkin. You're the object that Nedly is bound to. That's why you can see him, when no one else can. That's why he has to do whatever you say.'

Lil snorted. 'He never does what I say.' But then a memory poked its head round the corner of her mind, back in the doll hospital when they were fighting Grip. He had begged her not to make him go, but she had insisted that he leave, and so he did.

Lil looked up at Nedly and he looked back at her. Yossarian was still talking but they were both ignoring him until Lil suddenly interrupted. 'Hang on a minute, that doesn't make any sense; who would have bound us? There was no one there who could have done that when we met.' She folded her rubbery arms semi-successfully.

'Nedly bound himself to you.'

Lil tried to give Yossarian a disbelieving look but then she saw Nedly's face.

'I didn't mean to –' he began.

'He chose you,' said Yossarian at the same time. 'I don't know why but he did.'

'I'm sorry –' Nedly tried again.

'But why me?' Lil asked.

'I did it without thinking. I had been there in the bus station for so long I forgot why I was there, I forgot who I was, and then I saw you take the flyer. Do you remember? Babyface's flyer about losing Wool? No one else gave it a second glance. I couldn't even remember why it was important any more, only that it was.

You were going to help him, even though he was just a kid and it was only a toy.'

'Not just a toy to him,' whispered Lil.

'That's right – it was important to him. And it turned out it was important to everything.'

'Is that why you were at the bus station, because of the flyer?'

Nedly shrugged. 'I don't know how I ended up there. It just seemed like the right place to go . . .'

Yossarian interrupted. 'It's fascinating to see you commune with him, just like a regular conversation between two ordinary people.' He smiled. 'But I'm feeling a bit left out.' His smile widened. He had a lot of teeth and they were large and square like a horse's.

'Now, we need to have a serious grown-up talk,' he said to Lil. 'Being the only person who can see or hear a ghost is a big responsibility, too big for a child. But it's something we can look at and if I could find out how it happened, then maybe we can bind Nedly to someone else instead.'

'Someone else?'

'Sure, I mean, he has to be bound to something otherwise he would just disappear.' He sprang his fingers out into star shapes. 'Nedly, you don't want to be haunting Lil here all her life, do you? I mean it's all right now while you're still the same age but eventually she's going to grow up. And you won't.' His voice was gentle now. 'She's not going to want you hanging around for ever.' His expression grew pained. 'Can't you see how you would be holding her back?'

Nedly looked at Lil and then to his feet. His shoulders curled in and his head hung low, so that he shrank a little bit and the space he took up became smaller.

'Wait,' said Lil quickly. 'You don't speak for me. I don't think any of those things. Nedly, don't listen.'

'I can see she enjoys telling you what to do.' Yossarian gave a knowing nod.

'What?' Lil scowled at him. 'I mean, please don't listen, Nedly. He's twisting things. He doesn't know either of us. He's just trying to get you to . . .'

Yossarian raised his voice over hers. 'If he could be bound to someone old enough to really understand what they were taking on, someone who could work with him to grow his skills, a mentor.'

'Abe?' said Nedly.

Lil's eyes were narrowed and her jaw set. 'You mean someone like you,' she said to Yossarian.

'Who else?' Yossarian's own eyes gleamed greedily. 'You have your whole life ahead of you. You don't want to be stuck with a ghost, do you? Giving everyone the creeps . . .'

'I'm not stuck with him.' Lil glared at Yossarian. 'He's my friend.' She tried to talk to Nedly inside her head. 'We have to get out of here. He's dangerous, Nedly.' She tried to stand up but her rubbery legs wouldn't hold her. 'He just wants to control you.'

'The other thing worth keeping in mind . . .' Yossarian's voice was low and reasonable. 'Is that I can persuade the others to drop the whole Ghostcatching thing, or if not, I could just take him out of the city. I'm a grown up. I can do things like that.'

'Take him out of the city?' Lil murmured.

'To keep him safe.'

'No.' Lil's eyes had suddenly filled with tears that were impossible to see through. 'No!' she said more clearly, squeezing them out of the way. 'Nedly, don't listen. You need to get out of here. Just run, don't wait for me.'

Nedly backed slowly towards the tent flap.

'Telling him what to do again.' Yossarian tutted and typed in some numbers.

EGON's screen changed: a green grid covered it, stretched to mimic the form of the tent and broken only by a boy shape. Yossarian smiled warmly. 'Ah, there you are.' He looked round to face the spot where Nedly was standing. 'With this machine you're not invisible; EGON can see exactly where you are, all of the time. Who knows, if we really work at it there might even be a way to make you visible.'

Nedly stopped moving. His expression changed.

'Would you like that?' Yossarian rolled out a sympathetic bottom lip and nodded. 'I'll bet you would. Must be lonely being invisible.'

'I can see him,' said Lil.

Yossarian ignored her.

Lil stared at the tent flap. Abe was out there somewhere: she knew he was. It was only a matter of time before he burst into the tent and took care of Yossarian, and as soon as he did then Nedly could do the surge and take EGON out for good. They just had to wait a bit longer for him to find them.

'You're wondering where that sad sack old P.I. is?' Yossarian wheeled his chair into her sightline. 'I'm afraid he's gone. He threw in the towel.'

'No,' said Lil firmly. 'He would never do that.'

''Fraid so. You see, I needed some time alone with you, both of you, so I told a little lie. I told him you had gone back.'

'He wouldn't have believed you.'

Yossarian shrugged gently. 'So where is he?'

Lil looked at Nedly. 'Please, will you find him?'

Nedly hesitated.

'Not so fast!' Yossarian hit a switch and the green laser net sprang up on the walls. 'Don't panic. I won't use it unless you force me to. I just want you to stick around for long enough to have a proper chat. After that you can go whenever you like. I promise.'

Lil looked at his hands. 'You have your fingers crossed!' she objected.

Yossarian gave her a *what can you do* type shrug.

'ABE!' Lil shouted suddenly. 'Abe!!! If you can hear me. Help! Help! Mel-murpmph- murh-urbe!' Yossarian had whipped his orange cravat off and stuffed it into her mouth.

Nedly ran forward but was sprung back instantly by the elastic mesh of the grid.

'I don't want to hurt you, Deadly Nedly,' Yossarian said kindly. 'I just need you to hear me out.' He clamped his hand over Lil's mouth, resisting her numb fingers trying to prise it away. 'Noisy Lil here and that old has-been with the hat, they're both good people; they don't want to admit what a nuisance you are.' Nedly's eyes went to the floor. 'But I know you're so much more than that; you could have powers beyond your imagination. Work with me, Nedly Stubbs, and you'll never be a nuisance again.'

'URBE! URBE!' Lil continued to shout through the silk and hand. With barely concealed irritation Yossarian pulled out his paisley sash and wrapped it twice round Lil's mouth and then pulled the two ends tight. 'There now.' He knotted it and then fastened her hands behind her back with the ends. 'That's better.'

Chapter 22

Peace at Last

The green lights of the Projected Entrapment Matrix chequered the walls of the tent. Nedly stood in the middle of it, immobilised by fear and the cheese-wire laser beams.

'There,' said Yossarian, patting Lil on the head. 'I didn't want to do that but you just can't seem to keep your mouth shut, can you?'

Lil scowled at him from over the tightly wound sash.

Yossarian shrugged innocently. 'You forced

my hand, Lil Potkin. I'm one of the good guys. None of this was part of the plan but I underestimated how irritating you could be.' He reclaimed his seat in the operator chair and turned to face Nedly, smiling like a cat with its paw on a mouse. 'Now, where were we?'

Lil knew that Yossarian could see Nedly now, just as they had seen Grip back in the doll hospital, as a black shadow that broke up the lines of the grid. And just like Grip, Nedly was trapped in them: one flick of the switch and the net would spring into reverse, taking him with it. She had seen it happen, remembered how quick it was.

'The matrix is holding you fast, Deadly Nedly. There's no escaping it, I'm afraid,' said Yossarian. 'And I won't pretend that the means by which it would destroy you will be anything other than deeply unpleasant. BUT all is not lost – I could save you from that, no strings attached – ha! Well, some strings, obviously,' he laughed. 'But no bells.' He laughed again.

Lil's eyes bulged angrily. *There has to be a*

way out. It can't end like this; I won't let it – not without a fight. She tried to think hard, ignoring that the silk scarf had absorbed all the spit from her mouth and her fingers were growing numb.

Yossarian's eyes shone gleefully, reflecting the green lights. He held out his hand to where Nedly stood and beckoned him closer.

Lil leant forward, letting her feet take the weight of the chair, raised it several centimetres with her body and then put it down again a little way to the left.

Nedly! she thought as loudly as possible. He didn't react. *He doesn't want to look at me,* she thought. *Doesn't want me to see. Nedly!* she thought again. *Look at me, right now.* Yossarian could only see Nedly as a shadow but Lil could see how pale he was, that he was trembling, and that his eyes were dark and full of tears. Rage boiled and she had to swallow hard to stop her own tears from blinding her. He glanced sideways at her. *I know you can hear me, so listen: don't you*

dare give up now. I'm going to fix this, OK, but I need you to help me. I need you to distract him. Just keep his eyes on you. She leant forward again, shifted herself left and gained another few centimetres of ground.

Nedly stood, as unmoving as if he was carved of marble. His bony arms hung defeated at his side; he let his head drop down and then, very slowly, took a small step forward. Lil breathed out a sigh of relief; Yossarian's eyebrows went up in delight. He grinned at Nedly, like a father welcoming home his prodigal son.

Lil swivelled another few centimetres to her left. She was right alongside EGON now.

'Good choice,' Yossarian said, his eyes on Nedly as he shuffled closer. 'Excellent choice. That's right, just a bit nearer. EGON can take care of everything. I've already preprogrammed the formula.' He sighed happily and gave himself a hug. 'I knew you'd see it my way, in the end.'

Now! thought Lil, and Nedly suddenly ran at EGON, like a nocked arrow against a bowstring he stretched the lines of green light as he put everything he had into reaching the metallic shell. Lil pushed up with her toes, rocking backwards until the chair was on two legs and then leant left and let the whole show fall to the side. She landed with a *bumpf* on the spongy canvas floor. The Projected Entrapment Matrix grew thin as it expanded at the point that Nedly was trying to break through, and as if it sensed the danger EGON let out a high metallic whine.

Yossarian ducked, gave Nedly a look of bitter disappointment and roughly twisted one of EGON's dials to the max. The grid snapped back into shape, repelling Nedly into the centre of the room with an agonising groan.

'Now that was silly,' Yossarian chastised him. 'This equipment is very delicate. I hope you're not having second thoughts. I'm so looking forward to us working together.'

As Nedly struggled back onto his feet, he glanced over to the card table in the corner and saw what Yossarian had not yet seen. Lil had vanished. Nedly pulled himself up, until he was standing as tall as he could and took a deep breath.

From somewhere across the grounds a sharp, familiar bark sounded.

Yossarian couldn't see the slight glow that had risen in Nedly's skin, or the pulsing light that travelled towards his hands. He did notice the sharp increase in EM energy. 'What's this?' He tapped the screen. 'Where are you generating that energy from?'

He tutted and pressed some more buttons. 'Is it you . . . ?' The last word fell away as he stared at the place where Lil had been. He leapt to his feet and just had time to say 'Where –?' and then, with lightning speed, Margaret hurled herself through the tent flap and slid to a halt on the canvas floor.

She cast a quick worried glance up at Nedly and then turned up her hackles full blast, growling at Yossarian and baring every one of her small while teeth.

Yossarian peeled off an espadrille and tried

to swat her away with it. 'Lil!' Nedly yelled. 'Whatever you're going to do, do it now!'

Behind EGON Lil grabbed the thick red power cable and with all the strength she had in her almost dead hands, she braced her feet against the metallic shell and pulled.

It didn't budge.

Lil heaved again, gritting her teeth as hard as she could, and yanked it. The cable held fast.

A hulking bulge appeared in the silk wall of the tent. The bulge rolled sideways, grew a fist, which thrashed at the fabric, and then there was a tearing sound and the wall was rent apart with the edge of a pair of multi-use pliers.

Abe stumbled through it, blinking in the green light. Lil nearly swallowed the gag. He looked like he had gone fifteen rounds with a shrubbery: he was covered in mud, his hat was gone and so was one shoe; he had lost the sleeves of his mac and his tie was swivelled round to hang over his shoulder. Lil had never been so pleased to see him.

'Not so fast,' Abe slurred slowly, swinging his fist wildly at the air and then choking as the binoculars hula-hooped round his neck by their strap. They landed with a hard thump on his back and he swung round to answer the blow with one of his own.

Yossarian darted away from him, scowling. 'How did you wake up? Stay away from me – this is a very delicate operation – the wrong button here and it's goodnight, Deadly Nedly.'

Abe had untangled the binoculars and was holding them by the strap. 'I'll give you the wrong button.' He tried to grab for Yossarian's shirt but he was too far away to reach it and he swiped thin air, blinking in confusion.

'You're leaving me with no choice,' Yossarian insisted. 'If I can't have control over the Final Ghost, I'll make sure no one can!'

With a '*Murrgghhh!*' Lil tugged on the powerline with everything she had.

Yossarian reached for the switch. 'We could have made a good team,' he told the shadow of Nedly.

'NOOO!' yelled Abe, lurching for Yossarian but missing him by a good two metres. Momentum carried him stumbling behind EGON where he tried to hop to avoid Lil, got his foot caught on some kind of cable and went crashing to the floor.

Yossarian snorted and flicked the switch.

The green laser grid faltered and then it went out.

Yossarian looked at EGON, dumbfounded, and flicked the switch again a couple of times. Nothing happened.

Abe Mandrel knew a lucky break when he got one. He shook his head to clear it and whirled round to face Yossarian, swinging his binoculars like an Olympic hammer.

'What's going on –?' Yossarian peered round the side of the machine to see Lil glaring triumphantly back at him, the unplugged cable in one hand, and then, with a whoosh, Nedly caught him with a powerful blow, a bolt of spectral energy that lifted and spun him right off the ground. Yossarian landed, still twirling, straight into the path of Abe's binoculars. They poleaxed him right between the eyes. A surprised expression crossed his face and then he crumpled like a tissue-paper flower in the rain.

In the silence that followed, Lil, Abe and Nedly all held their breath. Only Margaret's panting could be heard above the rain. After a moment, when the threat of impending danger felt like it really had subsided, Abe dusted off the palm of his good hand on the leg of his muddy trousers, and held out his Swiss Army hand letter-opener to Lil, who used it to saw through the sash that bound her hands. She unwound it and spat out the peach cravat. Her mouth felt as dry as a stale bread roll.

Nedly was slumped against EGON, looking shaken. 'Are you OK?' Lil asked him. 'Are you hurt?'

'I'm OK. I think. Just a bit tuckered out.' He smiled back at her bleakly.

'Are *you* OK?' she asked Abe as together they pulled the unconscious Yossarian to his feet, dragged him to the camp bed and folded him into a seated position. He was slumped forward but his neck hung back and his mouth was open.

Abe sighed heavily and rubbed his collar. 'I've been better. This chump tried to knock me out with some kind of potion; he stabbed me in the neck with a needle full of it as soon as I poked my head round the door.

'I don't know how long I was out, but not for as long as he hoped; that so-called scientist must have underestimated how much body fat I have.

'I came to when Margaret stuck her wet nose in my eyes.' He paused to give Margaret's head fur a grateful rub and noticed that his mac was missing its sleeves. 'I suppose I must have stumbled around a bit trying to find you.

'Now, we don't have time for any more heroics tonight,' he growled. 'The rest of Ghostcatcher could be back at any minute. Nedly,' he addressed a random spot in the tent. 'You better split now, get a head start before they turn the fence back on.'

'But what about EGON?' Nedly protested. 'Shouldn't I try to –'

'Don't sweat it,' said Lil. 'We'll find another way. Just beat it for now, get away from here.'

He hesitated for a moment then gave her a quick smile and a nod, backed towards the flap and, with Margaret at his side, he ran.

Abe surveyed the tent. 'OK, grab your bag. This doesn't look good for us.' He nodded at Yossarian. 'We need to get some distance between us and the crime scene.' He held out his hand.

Lil didn't take it. 'Abe, we have to take EGON out now; this may be our only chance to stop him. Otherwise this was all for nothing. We'll never get back in again.'

'You go.' Abe dropped his chin. 'I'll take care of EGON.'

Lil shook her head. 'We'll do it together.'

They both stood staring at the impenetrable metallic shell. Lil flexed her fingers into a fist, picked up one of the folding chairs and broke it over EGON with a clang that reverberated through her teeth.

Abe winced at the sound. 'They'll hear us.'

Lil gave EGON a hard stare and shrugged. 'Let them come. If they're here with us, then they're not chasing Nedly.'

Abe nodded. 'All right, tough guy.' He squared up to EGON. 'Let's see what you've got.' He heaved up the operator chair left-handed and hurled it like a shotput into EGON's screen. A thin white crack appeared across the black surface. Abe gave Lil a grim smile. 'A start, but this is going to take some time.'

Lil rolled up her sleeves, Abe took off what was left of his coat and they got to work. After a few minutes they were battering him in perfect harmony, alternating blows like two woodcutters trying to take down a giant tree.

They laboured until every piece of furniture in the tent, except for the camp bed with Yossarian on it, had been smashed to pieces – but EGON had barely a mark.

Lil snatched up Gallows' hardback tome and threw it angrily at EGON's control panel. It simply bounced off. 'There must be a way to destroy it!' she yelled in frustration.

'There is,' replied a calm voice.

Magdalena Virgil stood in the mouth of the tent, frowning darkly.

'Professor Virgil –' Lil began, her Cryptic Eyebrow raised. 'We meet again.'

Virgil surveyed the mess with thinly pursed lips. 'I'm sure there's a perfectly good explanation as to why you're here.'

Abe nodded in agreement. His eyes searched the tent. There was a good explanation, but where had he left it?

'You two have been popping up all over the place. So I shouldn't really be surprised to find you here trying to destroy a piece of pioneering scientific equipment, behind a state-of-the-art security fence, in a top-secret research facility.'

She strode over to Yossarian, whose head still looked skyward, his mouth catching flies, prised apart his eyelids and then turned back to Lil. 'What happened to him?'

Lil offered up a grim smile and kept schtum.

'Let me take a guess. He was trying to stop you.'

It was one interpretation.

'Why?' she asked Abe.

It was Lil who answered. 'Because we don't want you to catch the Final Ghost, because he's got as much right to live in this city as any of us do.' She paused. 'But you know that, right? You know all about him.'

'No,' Virgil began slowly. 'I can't say we've –' She faltered. 'Look, Ghostcatcher has been contracted and commissioned by Acting Mayor Gordian to contain and dispose of the Final Ghost. Whatever and whoever that is, that's our job.'

Lil folded her arms. 'You don't always have to do what you're told. Not if you know it's wrong.'

'It's not always easy to tell what's right –'

'But sometimes it is.' Lil gave her the Squint.

'Everything you've seen over the last few weeks – do you really think the ghost is a threat? You have all the evidence, make a decision on the facts; you're a scientist, aren't you?'

Abe set his jaw and conjured up some of the old steel into his bleary eyes. 'But know this, if you do decide to continue to hunt this kid out of the city, even after all he's done to try to save it, you'll have to go through me. If I have to spend the rest of my life standing in your way, that's where I'll be.'

Lil planted herself beside him. 'That goes for me too.'

Virgil blew out her cheeks and sighed. There was a long moment of silence, and then she nodded as if to herself. Holding up one hand to show she meant no harm she plugged EGON in and flipped the switch. She laid her hand on the small metal circle that was cut into the surface and pushed it gently. A drawer popped out. Inside was a cartridge wrapped in circuitry.

'This is EGON's brain. It's where it stores the information on what the city looks like, what a ghost is and the energy levels that suggest electromagnetic activity, or hauntings. It took us weeks to calibrate it. If this was destroyed EGON would be useless, for a while at least.'

Lil reached out for it but Virgil didn't let go.

'If you're wrong, people could die. That ghost has a lot of power.'

Lil held on tightly. 'With all the power he has he's only ever used it for good. Could you say the same thing?'

Virgil flinched. 'I'm a scientist. I don't get involved in politics.'

'You're already involved,' Lil told her. 'We all are.'

Virgil's gaze softened; she almost smiled. She let go of the cartridge. 'You must have a lot of faith in him.'

'We're friends,' Lil told her. 'We have a lot of faith in each other.'

Abe nudged Lil with his elbow. 'I think that's what he might need right now, a friend. Leave this with me, kid. I'll take it from here. You go.' He swung his tie back straight, shuffled the knot towards his collar and tried to look reliable. He added gruffly, 'I won't let you down.'

Lil pressed the cartridge firmly into Abe's multi-purpose pliers and then took hold of his other hand and held on for a moment. 'I know.'

Lil made it to the phone box, drenched in sweat and mizzle. Minnie, Babyface and Margaret were in there waiting. Minnie opened the door and Lil bundled in, Babyface squashed himself into the corner to make room.

Minnie stopped her gum-chewing to say: 'You made it!' She squinted back down the lane. 'Where's Abe?'

Lil bent down to rub Margaret's head. 'He's still there, talking things through with Ghostcatcher.'

Babyface frowned. 'Does he need a rescue?'

Lil smiled distractedly at him. 'Not this time. Abe can handle it.'

The little boy looked over the almost

non-existent space around Lil. 'Where's Nedly? Is he safe? Is he here?'

'No,' said Lil. 'I mean, yes, he's safe, for now.' She looked out across the black fields towards the city. 'But I don't know where he is, so I'm going to find him.'

Chapter 23

This Bitter Earth

Even in the very early hours of morning, downtown Peligan City did not sleep. The centre was still a circus of gold casino buildings, glittering billboard advertisements and cascading electronic tunes. Taxis crawled along bumper to bumper, horns blaring in a never-ending chain of headlights.

It was a storm of colour and noise and Lil was in the eye of it. Small but bright in her signature yellow rain mac she stood alone beneath the skyscrapers that stretched up beyond the lights like bare trees in a dark and impenetrable forest.

Lil was thinking hard. She could call Nedly to her – she had done it before, she realised, without meaning to. She had called him all the way back from wherever Grip had taken him; he had followed her voice like the sound of bells. Just a few words and he would be there. Maybe she wouldn't even have to say them; maybe she could just think them?

But that would be against his will and now she knew better. She was going to find him the hard way, whatever it took. As EGON had been dismantled – for now at least – she was the only person who could.

Squinting through the rain she tried to imagine where he would run to. It was hard to be alone in Peligan City, where there were people on every corner, under every bridge and behind every door. Where could you go to get some space?

Above her one building dominated the sky,

stretching up like a glass-fronted behemoth; it darkly reflected the dazzle of the casinos that surrounded it. Lil let her gaze rise over its slippery carapace until she was looking skyward and a fat drop of rain hit her in the eye.

On the rooftop of City Hall, Nedly sat on the edge of a plinth upon which stood a stone statue of a huge winged lion with massive paws and a mane frozen in mid-flow. Its enormous stone face was tilted down to look out across the city.

From far away he heard the puff and shunt of a train in the distance. It sounded just like breath or, more exactly, like someone out of breath. The sound grew louder and closer until it felt like it was right behind him. Slowly Nedly turned round and a sweaty figure in a yellow mac flumped down at his side.

His jaw dropped open. 'How did you get up here?'

Lil held a finger up while she fought to regain her breath, and then wheezed, 'It was tough.

I've been climbing for almost an hour. I didn't think I was going to make it along that ledge.'

'What! You could have fallen off!' Nedly's eyes were the size of saucers.

'I'm kidding. I took the fire-escape stairs – all of them,' she added grimly.

Nedly hung his head. 'I just wanted to be on my own for a bit.'

'I know. I just wanted to pop up for a minute and let you know I was about, if you changed your mind about being on your own, I mean.'

He gave her a small smile.

Huddled under the chest of the stone lion they watched the rain pour down, falling past them like dashes, blurring the lines of the buildings below. Lil put up her hood and hooked one arm round the lion's sturdy leg so she could lean forward and look over the city.

From so high above you couldn't see the rubbish or the dirt; even the air smelt cleaner. Peligan City looked like a cluster of man-made stalagmites, a crystal garden of black shapes and scattered jewels with car headlights roving like fireflies and the Kowpye River cutting through it all like a satin ribbon.

'It looks better from up here. Do you reckon we could see our house?'

Nedly squinted into the darkness 'Maybe, if you had binoculars.'

'If only Abe were here . . .' Lil grinned. 'Anyway, it would probably just look like all the others.'

'How did you know where I was?'

'I had a hunch.' Lil raised her eyebrow cryptically.

'Really?'

'No, I've been looking all night. It was just luck – and maybe a bit of a hunch too.'

They both stopped speaking and looked out at the city. Beyond the centre the rooftops flattened out, with just the odd car prowling the streets, and then further out they could see the snaking trains, the lit metros and the hulking freight wagons that tramped along the city lines on their way to the docks. Slow-moving clouds

billowed from the industrial chimneys, rolling out like foam and then growing soft as they dispersed and then . . . Who knew what lay beyond, but the blue-grey light of dawn was already at the horizon, a horizon Lil had never seen before – but then she had never been this high above the city.

'So . . .' she said, glancing sidelong at Nedly.

'So?' he replied.

'What now?'

'I was thinking maybe I'd skip town for a while.' He looked across at the horizon line.

'You can't leave, not now!'

He gave her a dark look. 'Can't I?'

Lil looked mortified. 'That's not what I meant,' she said quickly. 'You know it isn't. I would never mean it like that. Never.' She shook her head. 'What I meant was, please don't go.'

Nedly took a deep breath and frowned. 'Then everyone could just forget about me. It would be like I never existed and you wouldn't have to keep trying to convince everyone that I'm not real.' Lil's jaw dropped in protest but Nedly continued, 'I heard you talking to your mum that night.'

Lil felt her ears burning red. 'I – I just thought it would be safer, not better. I wanted people to leave you alone. I didn't think –'

'No,' he agreed, his gaze bent on his scuffed old trainers. 'You didn't think. Not about how that would feel for me.'

Lil looked down at her own boots. 'I'm sorry.'

'I wish that people could see the real me; not just a spook that gives everyone the creeps. I only wanted the chance to be someone good, like everyone else has. That's all I ever wanted.' Nedly shrugged, his pale skin had taken on the shadows of night. 'But look at all the trouble I've caused. Peligan City would be better off without me.' A ghostly tear dropped from his eye and vanished.

Lil snorted. 'Trouble! Are you serious? Peligan City would be haunted by the most terrifying band of spooks if not for you! Lots of people would actually be dead, not to mention we would have Cornelius Gallows as mayor. When I think about what might have been . . .' She shuddered. 'I don't even want to think about it.

'Just stick around, things will change,' Lil pleaded. 'You'll see.'

'Not for me,' Nedly said quietly, and then an edge crept into his voice. 'Things will never change for me. This is me now. For ever.'

'Not for ever,' Lil reminded him quietly. 'Just as long as I'm around.'

Nedly flickered, his eyelids dipped as his head hung down.

'Yossarian said you'd never be free of me.'

'When did I ever say that I wanted to be free of you? They were his words not mine. You're my best friend! You know he was telling you that stuff because he wanted to make trouble. He wanted us to split so he could bind you to himself and make you do what he wanted.'

'I know.'

'So why were you listening? He was trying to make you feel down on yourself so you'd make a bad decision. You can't let people get to you like that.'

'But he was right: I do give people the creeps.'

'So what?'

He shrugged. 'So it's not a good feeling.'

Lil gripped the lion's leg tighter and swivelled perilously to face him. 'Nedly, you can't let other people decide who you are, that's something you have to work out for yourself. If you do decide to go, go because you want to, but not because of me, or anyone else in this town, because for the record I want you to stay, and what the people who don't know you think doesn't matter.'

She dug her heels into the ledge for balance then reached her spare hand out and laid it over Nedly's, letting it sink slightly through. It felt like freshly fallen snow. But Nedly didn't react or say anything.

'What about Peligan City – don't you want to stay and fight for it?' Lil asked desperately.

He narrowed his eyes. 'I'm not sure it's worth fighting for any more.'

Lil looked up into the stone lion's grave face; standing on its plinth it looked weary, as though it had been watching for a long time. She wondered if it was tired too.

'You don't mean that.' She squeezed her eyes shut to push out the tears and let the rain wash them away and then she took a deep breath. 'You know, back when we had McNair, people had someone to get behind. That's what Peligan City needs more than anything now, someone to believe in. Why shouldn't that be you?'

Nedly almost laughed. 'Because I'm dead, OK? I'M DEAD!' He shouted this so loudly that a spectral wind gusted around Lil, whipping her hair into her eyes and dislodging the pencil she was keeping there. It bounced through Nedly and rolled over the edge.

'I know,' Lil yelled back. 'I know you're dead. I mean, you're a ghost – I don't think it's the same thing and anyway.' She crooked her arm over her face to shield it from the wind; the rain turned into sleet as it neared them. 'That's just one of your . . . qualities. It's not what defines you; it's what you do that makes you who you are.'

But Nedly was on a roll. 'What do you think I'm going to do? If you're thinking of all these things that *you're* going to do, like grow up and find a job and live in a house of your own – that's not going to happen for me!'

The stone leg of the lion had turned bone-achingly cold but Lil clung on fiercely as the creeps hammered in her chest.

'I know . . . I know!' she shouted into the gale. You're right!'

'What!'

'Everything you just said. I'm agreeing with you.'

The wind dropped. Nedly glared at Lil with tear-filled eyes, and then wiped them angrily away with the back of his hand and stared out across the city.

Lil's teeth were chattering and her fingers were numb so she took a deep sigh to try to slow her breathing down and then said: 'So, what now?'

'What do you mean?'

'Because that's the only question that matters – you can't do anything about the things that have already happened. It's what you do next that counts.'

'What can I do?' He shrugged helplessly.

Lil shook her head in disbelief. 'Things no one else can. Nedly, you can walk through walls, move things without touching them. You're invisible, you can generate electricity and use it . . . and above all, you're the bravest and kindest person I know. So, if you ask me – which you did, actually – you *could* be the thing that this city needs. Something it has needed for a really long time. You could be a real hero.'

Nedly smirked humourlessly. 'Yeah, one that everyone was terrified of.' He looked down at the scratch on the back of his hand, the one that had never healed, the one he had got the night he died. 'Some things you can't change, no matter how much you try.'

Below in the city the street lights started to

go out, one by one, and there on the horizon they saw a pale glow, as though the fabric of night had faded there, and then a thin, bright line, a seam of precious metal spilled into a luminous pool, the edge of the sunrise.

'So that's what it looks like.' Nedly stared at it.

'It's really something.' Lil rubbed the tears out of her eyes.

They watched the sun as it alighted on the city, glinting off the edges of the buildings, like gold leaf. The light danced over Lil's cheeks, and she closed her eyes and let the soft glow warm her skin before she spoke.

'I'm not giving up on you, Nedly.'

He looked at her, tears still haunting his eyes. Lil's own eyes filled again too when she looked back at him. 'Whatever it takes, we're going to fix this so you can stay. I promise.'

Nedly grinned lopsidedly and then his face became serious again. 'If anyone can, then it's you.'

'Ha!' Lil gulped noisily. A tear had escaped

and was hanging below her nose. She snorted and then a thought occurred to her; she wiped the tear away absent-mindedly and a gleam came to her eye. Lil's dangling legs began to tap at the thin air. She pulled her spare pencil out from a pocket and started chewing on it. After a moment she got to her feet and said, 'I have to go.'

'Now?' Nedly looked crestfallen.

'There's something I need to do.' There was a silence in which Lil did not say, *Do you want to come too?* 'Will you be OK?'

Nedly grinned but his eyes didn't catch it. 'I'll be fine. I'll probably just sit up here for a bit longer.'

'OK.' She started towards the fire escape and then stopped. 'Just don't give up. Not yet. Promise me you won't leave, not for a couple of days at least.'

Lil didn't wait for an answer. She had a job to do.

Chapter 24

The Whole Truth

An hour later Lil walked into the Nite Jar Cafe. The early breakfast crowd were on their way out, leaving behind them the smell of hot coffee and toasted bread.

Velma was standing at the counter, wearing her hair curled up under a mint-green headscarf with a poodle fringe. She raised her eyebrows expectantly. 'Did we do all right?'

Lil gave her a heartfelt smile. 'You were ace.'

Velma nodded over at a corner booth. Naomi Potkin was waiting there with two cups of hot chocolate. Like Lil, she had dark shadows under her eyes and looked pale and tired.

Lil peeled off her mac and slid into her seat looking contrite. 'I'm sorry I worried you.' She stirred her hot chocolate, closing her heavy eyes for a moment to let the sweet warm steam drift over her face.

'According to Abe you were out looking for a friend, is that right?'

Lil nodded. 'I found them.'

'Good.' Naomi leant in and lowered her voice. 'Marsha Quake has been looking for you all night; there was a big development in the Ghostcatcher story.' She continued whispering at speed, her gaze fixed on Lil. 'Coincidentally last night, while you were off looking for a friend, Ghostcatcher were called out to a suspected haunting here at the Nite Jar; meanwhile, back on Bun Hill, an unidentified group of burglars incapacitated the alarm system and broke into Rorschach Laboratories, sabotaging an extremely expensive piece of pioneering scientific equipment.

'Only, Quake has heard from a source in the P.D. that the lead scientist there, Professor Virgil, isn't seeking to press charges against the perpetrators. Instead, she has resigned from her post, but not without tipping us off that City Hall Waste Disposal Services have been dumping the toxic by-product of some mineral called black tourmaline, which Ghostcatcher had been using, on the outskirts of Peligan, contaminating the soil and killing all the vegetables in the orphanage allotments – which solves my story. And she has vowed to use her considerable intellect and scientific knowledge to prove it and is petitioning City Hall to pay for the clean-up operation.'

She paused to take a breath. 'So it looks like someone had a busy night.'

Lil nodded sagely. 'Yes, it does.'

'And nothing I just said made you raise so much as an eyebrow.'

Lil quickly raised an eyebrow, but it was too

late. 'I didn't know about the contaminated soil,' she said quietly.

Naomi sighed. 'I thought we were on the same team now?'

Lil buried her eyes in the hot chocolate. 'We are. I just couldn't explain what was going on before. I wanted to.'

Naomi creased up her forehead. 'Whatever it was, you could have trusted me.'

'I know.' Lil took a deep breath. 'I'm going to start now. Did you bring it?'

Naomi nodded to the seat beside her where, wrapped up in an old pillowcase, was Lil's Olympia SM-3 typewriter. 'Are you going to tell me what all this is about?'

'Yes,' said Lil earnestly. She gulped a big swig of chocolate and swallowed it nosily. 'I need your help, with a story.'

Naomi smiled and her tired eyes crinkled. 'OK.'

'But I'm worried you won't believe me.'

'I'll believe you. But if this is something you want to put into print it's not me you'll need to convince. Tell me everything, from the beginning.'

And so Lil Potkin ordered a plate of raisin whirls and another two hot chocolates and her mother sat in silence while Lil told her the truth; the whole story from beginning to end, which started at the Paradise Street All-Night Bus Station, and ended on the rooftop of City Hall.

When she had finished, Lil picked up of one of the untouched pastries and took a big bite. While she chewed it her mother just stared at her, with a slight frown pinching her eyebrows together. Lil swallowed half her mouthful and spoke through the rest of it. 'What do you think?'

Naomi's hot chocolate had grown cold and a skin had formed on the surface. She pushed it to one side. 'It's a great story. Is it really true?'

'Every word.'

Naomi picked up a raisin whirl and pointed it at Lil. 'Can you prove it?'

Lil exhaled and her shoulders drooped uncertainly. 'I don't know.'

Naomi studied her daughter's pale face, her worse-for-wear yellow mac and the stub of a chewed pencil she had stuck in her hair, and then she took hold of her hand across the table and squeezed it. 'We better make some calls. We'll need someone to go on the record, someone solid. And if we can get it past Logan, there are some practical delivery details we'll need to take care of.'

She held her hand up to Velma for a pot of strong coffee. 'It's going to be a long day.'

They wrote the story right there in the Nite Jar. Naomi scoured the Peligan City phone directory and made the calls from the phone by the counter; interviews were held in the corner booth. Lil made two runs to the library for further fact-checking, then took her turn phoning round, twiddling her pencil expertly like a baton and snapping it into action against her reporter's notebook when she needed to.

Velma and Yoshi came back and forth with coffee and sandwiches, the windows of the Nite Jar grew steamier, interviews took place back to back and a small queue formed along the counter of people waiting to take their seat in the booth.

By mid-afternoon, Lil's notebook was full and she had chewed her way through six pencils. She typed up what they had so far and handed it to Naomi to read.

As Naomi turned over the last page she laid her palm on top of the pile and smiled. 'We've done it, Lil. It's a good piece. Possibly the best.'

With the pages stuffed safely under her camelhair coat they left the Nite Jar and stepped out into the rain.

At the library they stood side by side and knocked on the door of the librarian's office. When Lil presented Logan with the manuscript she received no more than a quizzical look in return.

Lil started to explain what they were trying to do as they followed her to the desk but the librarian and editor of the *Klaxon* raised a finger to silence her.

'The story has to stand on its own two feet now,' Naomi explained.

Logan flipped the switch on the Anglepoise lamp that hung over her desk, sat down in her cane office chair, which creaked as she leant back, and stuck her feet on the table, legs crossed at the ankle. As she read the first line her eyebrows went up behind the green-framed spectacles. Her gaze ping-ponged between Lil and Naomi for a couple of passes and then dipped back to the manuscript.

At the bottom of the page she licked her finger and thumb and sent the top sheet to the back of the pile and then continued until she had read them all. Lil and Naomi watched her anxiously.

When Logan had finished, she took a deep breath, looked at them in turn, sighed, shook her head and took her feet off the desk. Then she scooted her chair in, took a pencil out of her shirt pocket, licked the end and began to annotate the text with her bizarre alphabet of correction marks. Lil felt Naomi's hand squeeze hers.

Naomi took the edited document from Logan and showed it to Lil with a grin. 'Do you want to type this up or shall I?'

Lil typed as Naomi dictated. Once they had their final copy Naomi pulled the last page out of the typewriter roll and added it to the others. 'Read it through carefully,' she advised Lil, handing the pages back to her in a neat pile. 'We only have one shot at this.'

Lil read through the article with a mixture of feelings, most notably thrill and dread. At the end her eyes went back to the title and to the names below it.

A report by Stellar Darke and Randall Collar

It was what she had always hoped for, there in black and white. She jigged her knee, tapping her foot restlessly against the floor, took a breath and then fed the newsprint and carbon paper back through typewriter roller and wound it to the top of the page. She nudged it until it was in place and then stamped hyphens right through names. She rolled down a line and then began typing again.

When she had finished she showed it to her mother who looked gravely at Lil over the top of her spectacles.

'There will be no coming back from this.'

'I know,' said Lil. 'But I think it's time.'

When Lil fell asleep at long last, tucked up in a bundle of coats on a line of chairs in a quiet corner of the library, the press was already at work on the bumper print run ready for the morning delivery. She was woken gently long before the sun came up, handed her mac and a parcel of papers, and along with everyone else she took to the streets of Old Town to make her round.

Abe, Naomi, Babyface, Mr Kolchak, Minnie, Irving Starkey and Velma all took routes on top of the usual delivery crew. This time no flyers for the Black Pug Eatery were used. Yoshi took a bundle of papers to the Nite Jar and posted them all along Spooner Row.

By 9 a.m. they had run out. Lil stumbled back to Angel Lane like a sleepwalker, fed Waldo some seeds, refilled his water, then crawled into bed and slept.

Chapter 25

The Definite Article

Lil woke late. She wrestled on her dressing gown and padded down the attic stairs. She stopped on the landing outside the bathroom, but the airing cupboard was empty. She stared into the piles of sheets and towels as a train rattled past, joggling the slatted wooden shelves and making the folded flannels tremble. She held her breath without meaning to as the racing heartbeat of the locomotive engine passed, the wheels clattering urgently against the track, and then in the quiet that followed she whispered, 'Nedly?'

There was no answer.

The morning's edition of the *Herald* was lying face down on the mat where it had fallen, her mum's coat was still hanging on the rack and Waldo was going hell for leather on his wheel as Lil walked down the hallway towards the kitchen, following the familiar smell of toast.

Naomi looked up and grinned as Lil walked in. 'Good morning, little love! You're just in time. We're making breakfast . . . together. Me and Nedly.'

There he was, sitting on the counter. Nedly beamed at Lil and she beamed back.

'You can see him?' she said, puzzled and relieved in equal measure, and then with a smile breaking across her face, 'You can see him!'

'No, Lil,' Naomi cut in quickly. 'I can't see him, I –' She exhaled. 'We're muddling through.' She gave Lil a kiss on the forehead and murmured, 'He's by the toaster, right?'

Lil nodded.

'I pushed the toast down,' said Nedly proudly. 'It's just, you know, toasting.' He shrugged casually.

'Great.' Lil's eyes were glued to the impossible but completely normal-looking scene of Nedly making breakfast with her mother. After a couple of minutes the toasting smell darkened to something more potent.

'I think it's done,' Naomi said brightly, looking at an empty spot in the kitchen. Nedly tried making it pop up, jabbing at it with a glowing finger until both slices were suddenly ejected and soared over his head, leaving a trail of smoke. Naomi caught one; the other hit the floor in an explosion of crumbs.

'It's all right,' said Lil, swiping it off the lino. 'Waldo can have that bit. So, what's going on?'

'Nedly and I have had a talk,' Naomi said, filling the teapot and putting it on the table with a bottle of milk and some cutlery. 'Well, I talked and he listened.' She frowned. 'I *hope* he listened.'

'I listened,' Nedly chipped in, expertly

straightening up the knife so that it lay parallel to the butter dish. 'Then I did some talking but your mum couldn't actually hear me – she just stared at this cobweb on the other side of the room that was blowing about in the draught from the window, but it didn't matter because I think she knew what I wanted to say because then she suggested we should make breakfast together.'

'OK,' said Lil, then she dropped her voice and murmured, 'Do you want me to translate anything?'

'No, I think it's OK.'

'So,' said Naomi. 'I have to head into the office; I should probably empty my desk before they take away my security clearance. I'll leave you two to catch up. Oh –' She paused and then added off-handedly, 'By the way, I invited Abe round for dinner this evening.'

'Great,' said Lil.

'Yep,' said Naomi, rushing off into the hall to get her coat and then coming back to put it on. 'So, he's coming over. I'll probably do spaghetti bolognese.' She paused, one arm in the coat sleeve while her ears turned from pink to cherry red. 'Do you think that's the best one to do?'

'It's your speciality,' Lil confirmed.

Naomi nodded, pulled Lil into a lock and kissed the top of her head. 'OK then. I'll catch you, both, later.'

She laid the morning's edition of the *Klaxon* on the table with a significant look, and left.

When they heard the front door slam Nedly slumped down on the kitchen chair. 'Phew! That was A-MAZING! I'm going to have to work on some kind of code for the future but what a morning! You should have seen it; she totally caught me by surprise – we were just sitting there listening to the radio and I must have caused a bit of interference or something because it went to static for a second and she suddenly just said, 'Nedly? Are you there?''

His excitement was contagious. Lil drew up a chair of her own. 'What did you say back?'

Nedly shrugged expansively. 'Nothing, well nothing she could hear. I just knocked over a cereal box. It's all I could think of. But it worked! We communicated like that for a while; knocking it over was "yes", not knocking it over was "no". It's not perfect but it's definitely the basis of something.'

He let his shoulders relax, contentment gleaming in his eyes. 'How did you convince her that I was real?'

'I had help,' Lil admitted.

She pulled out a chair for Nedly to take a seat and then pushed the morning edition of the *Klaxon* across the table and swivelled it to face him. 'Check this out. It's a big scoop.'

The Truth about the Final Ghost
by Lil Potkin and Naomi Potkin

It was front-page news, and the first time a *Klaxon* reporter had put their own name to a big story since the death of McNair. He glanced up at Lil, and she saw that there was fear in his round, dark eyes.

'It's OK,' she said. 'Just read it.'

For weeks Peligan City has lived in fear, fear of the Final Ghost. Described by the Herald *as a terrifying spectre 'too powerful to be allowed to roam freely', and hunted relentlessly by Ghostcatcher, the Final Ghost has evaded capture for months. But what do we really know about him, and what does he want with us?*

The Klaxon *has gained unique and exclusive access to the Final Ghost and in the following pages we will lay before you information about his past, his death and his afterlife, including interviews with eyewitnesses, experts and those who know him best, his friends.*

But the first thing you should know is his name. The Final Ghost is Ned 'Nedly' Stubbs, he's eleven years old and he was a victim of crime, not a perpetrator.

Nedly looked up at Lil, his eyes glistening. 'Go on,' she said, and he continued reading.

Early Life

Ned Stubbs was born right here in Peligan City. He never knew his parents: he was left at the Hawks Memorial Orphanage on Bun Hill when he was only a baby, and he lived there for all of his young life.

Orphanage caretaker Mr Emil Kolchak described young Ned as 'a quiet and good-natured boy, who was kind and helpful, and always looking out for the smaller kids.'

One of the orphans in question, seven-year-old Clark Kennedy, was a particular friend of Stubbs'. 'Ned would share whatever sweets he had with me. He knew toffees were my favourite and sometimes he would save up and get those ones, even though he didn't really like them. He was my hero.'

Nedly's eyes filled with tears. He had to blink them away before he could read on.

Death

So how did this kind young orphan become a ghost in the first place? Who killed him, and why?

Ned Stubbs was murdered by the evil genius and ex-Lucan Road mobster Cornelius Gallows in the ruins of Rorschach Asylum over one year ago.

The old asylum lies less than a mile away from the orphanage. Once a refuge for those suffering torments of the mind, it had been burned down ten years earlier in a mysterious fire that claimed the lives of several staff and inmates, including, it was believed, Cornelius Gallows and his young acolyte, the teenage arsonist, Leonard Owl.

In fact, both had survived the blaze and had been hiding out in the asylum ever since while Gallows perfected his experimental procedure to weaponise a ghost.

Gallows had set his mind on conquering Peligan City. He stayed under the radar for

364

the next ten years, as a man who officially did not exist, a situation he would exploit time and again, beavering away in the shadows until finally he was ready to turn Leonard Owl into his first experimental subject: Mr Glimmer.

It was on that fateful night that Nedly Stubbs crossed their paths.

Stubbs had strayed into the asylum on the lookout for a lost toy. Clark Kennedy remembers: 'I lost my best toy, Wool. I didn't think I could sleep without it. But Ned went over to fetch it back from the asylum even though it was dark and haunted and we're never supposed to go there. Just to help me out.'

It was there in the asylum that Stubbs came across Gallows' gruesome experiment and attempt to murder Leonard Owl. Stubbs tried to stop him, but little did he know that the procedure was already underway. So it was that the very night Gallows transformed Leonard Owl into Mr

Glimmer, who became known to us all as the Firebug Killer, a second ghost was created: that of Nedly Stubbs.

Unlike Owl, Stubbs was not bound to Gallows' will and so he escaped from the doctor's clutches and tried to find help. It took him a while but eventually he succeeded. It was Nedly Stubbs working in collaboration with local detective agency Mandrel Investigations, who were responsible for ending the escapades of the Firebug Killer. When all attempts to solve the crimes evaded police, Stubbs provided the vital information needed to solve the case, not to mention aiding the exposure and eventual capture of our disgraced former mayor and ex-mobster Ramon Le Teef.

Absolom 'Abe' Mandrel, who worked with Nedly on the Gallows/Le Teef case, had this to say: 'I've worked with Stubbs on several cases. He's got a keen eye and a big heart and he's saved my neck a couple of times. Sure, the kid is different, but he's got guts. He puts himself out for people, even though he's had a tough time of it. He doesn't let that hold him back.'

But Gallows wasn't done with Peligan City yet. No sooner was Le Teef arrested than the 'evil genius' vanished again, only to turn up masquerading as prison doctor Alector Lankin, and safely locked away in Fellgate Prison. Was it a coincidence that prisoners began to die in a mysterious epidemic shortly after, and then that a series of bizarre murders and strange deaths swept the city? A crime wave that was for the most part ignored by the authorities until they had the means to end it.

When amateur ghost hunter Irving Starkey gave the Klaxon *the scoop to break the Haunting of Peligan City story he was concerned that the public were being kept in the dark about the spooks on the loose.*

'I had always wanted to make contact with visitors from the afterlife but the grade

1 spectral manifestations that were plaguing Peligan City were another kettle of fish. People were dying, I only saw the harm that was being done, not the good. It wasn't until later that I saw that not all the spooks were the same. When I met Nedly Stubbs, the Final Ghost, I was most struck by his kindness and his decency to forgive a foolish man who could not see the wood for the trees.'

Long before Ghostcatcher turned up on the scene it was Ned Stubbs working with Mandrel Investigations who dispatched all but one of Gallows' deadly spooks to end the reign of terror.

Mandrel recalls, 'Young Ned went hand to hand with some of the most dangerous criminals this city has ever known. He showed more courage than anyone I know. I trust this kid and I'm proud to know him.'

* * *

Nedly gulped hard. His whole body was glowing softly, filling the kitchen with a warm pearly light. He looked up at Lil and she gave him an encouraging grin.

Twice Nedly Stubbs has helped to save Peligan City from the spectral forces that have plagued it, but still he has been hunted while the Herald *stoked up fear and anger towards him, and although the story sold lots of papers, the truth is that no malevolent action by any spectre has taken place since the capture of Gallows' last weaponised ghost, Mr Grip. Since Gallows himself was found dead on that very night and all his equipment seized it's likely that no further spooks were created. So why are Ghostcatcher still chasing the Final Ghost?*

Magdalena Virgil, lead scientist of Ghostcatcher made this statement: 'It is true that we have been tracking the Final Ghost for weeks and we have come very close to capturing him, but our research into who he was and his nature has caused us to call off our pursuit. We have confirmed the identity of the Final Ghost as that of Ned Stubbs and have found no evidence that his spirit is any threat to the public. If our research suggests anything, it is that we should be thanking Stubbs, not fighting him.'

Acting Mayor Pam Gordian refused to confirm or deny that the Final Ghost was still of interest to City Hall but was unable to produce any records to prove that either the crime rate or the death rate had remained high following the entrapment of Mr Grip at the doll hospital in the Old Town – in fact, the Klaxon *has seen evidence from their source at the Police Department that the serious crime level has actually gone down over the last few weeks. Peligan City P.D. also reported that their alleged investigation into the so-called Fright File had been closed.*

So what now for this unusual young hero?

We managed to make contact with Nedly Stubbs and he had this to say: "I wish that people could see the real me; not just a spook that gives everyone the creeps. I just wanted the chance to be someone good, like everyone else has. That's all I've ever wanted.'

Citizens of Peligan City, it's over to you.

Nedly kept his eye on the last page, elbows propped on the table with the heels of his hands resting against his cheekbones. Lil watched him expectantly.

Finally he whispered in a husky voice, 'It's a good story.' He glanced shyly up at her. 'Do you think anyone will read it?'

'A copy has gone into every home in Old Town.'

'I can't believe everyone said all that nice stuff about me.' His pale cheeks blushed a pinkish grey.

Lil gave the pot a stir and then poured out the tea. 'People think a lot of you.'

Nedly sat on his hands and jigged his legs under the table. 'Is it safe, though, publishing it under your own names?'

'I just thought, maybe it was time we all stopped hiding. Gordian said she was going to make this city better – someone needs to hold her accountable.'

Nedly grinned. 'And that's you?'

'Me, Mum, Marsha, Abe, Logan, Minnie, Irving Starkey. I bet there are other people who think it's time things got changed and are prepared to try to change them.' She looked up hopefully, a piece of blackened toast halfway to her mouth. 'You?'

Nedly rubbed his chin thoughtfully. 'Well, I'm a hero of Peligan City now, so . . . I'm going to have to check my diary.'

Lil rolled her eyes. 'Don't let it go to your head.'

Nedly wrapped his glowing fingers round the glass milk bottle and then, staring at it very intently, lifted it three inches off the table, tilted it so that a thin line of white liquid trickled out and into Lil's tea and shakily returned it to the table. He let out a sigh of relief and said, 'Things might actually work out in the end.'

'They might,' Lil agreed, taking a bite out of the toast.

Nedly thought for a moment, cleared his throat momentously and said in a deeper voice than normal, 'After all, it's not who I am but what I do that matters.'

Lil gave him a pitying look. 'I'm not going to quote everything you say now. That story was just a one-off.'

Nedly sagged. 'I thought it sounded pretty good.'

Lil shoved the last bit of toast in her mouth and shook her head as she chewed. 'It sounded exactly like a line from one of your comic books.'

Nedly shrugged one shoulder. 'I'm still going to use it.'

'S'up to you.' Lil brushed the crumbs off her fingers, carefully placed the knife across the plate and then asked, 'So what now?'

Nedly interlaced his fingers and gave his arms a stretch. 'Right now?'

'Yeah.' Lil felt the tips of her ears growing warm. 'What you were saying on the roof of City Hall, about going away for a while. About leaving?'

Nedly looked at her gravely. 'I could really never leave you.' Lil returned the look with a bashful smile. 'No, I mean,' he continued, 'even if I wanted to.' Lil's smile slipped. 'That's what Yossarian was saying. But I think I do need to spend some time alone.' He tried to say the next bit as quickly as he could. 'To find myself or something, just for a little while.'

Lil kept her eyes on the table and nodded. 'Of course.' She paused and then added, 'I suppose I just got used to having you around.'

'You'll be OK?' Nedly said anxiously.

'Yeah,' said Lil. 'Of course. It's no big deal. And maybe if I needed your help, with something serious or I missed you a lot, I could call and you would come back – right?'

'Whenever you needed me.' Nedly grinned.

Lil grinned back. 'Same here.'

'Hang on – it doesn't work like that.'

'Yeah, it does.' Lil took a big gulp of tea. 'We just need to work it out. You might have to actually call, maybe learn how to haunt the telephone line or something like that.'

Nedly shrugged happily. 'I'll see what I can do.'

Epilogue

One Month Later

On the corner of Spooner Row, newsagent Julius Oliver pulled down the grey metal shutter on his kiosk and padlocked it to the ground. He paused for a second, listening. It was long past dark and the streets had a lonely feel, but not an empty one. Grey steam rose from the drains and floated thinly over the wet pavement like rafts of mist in a graveyard.

Julius pulled his woollen hat down low and shoved his hands deep into his pockets where they could rest protectively on the thin bundle of notes zipped into the money belt round his belly under his patched jacket. Head down and eyes on his feet, he started walking.

A streetlight overhead buzzed and the light dimmed. An empty can rolled into the gutter on a breeze he couldn't feel.

He reached the junction and stepped out into the road without looking; the blare of a horn rang out. Julius recoiled, his heart hammering as the car prowled away. It had no lights. He watched it go until the last glint of grey metal had vanished past the street lamps.

Turning up the collar on his jacket he started walking again, faster this time. He heard a noise on the wind, the low growl of an engine moving slowly. He made a left, down beside the old waste ground, and skirted the chain-link fence for a block. He was almost out at the other side when he saw the car pull up ahead, blocking the lane. Julius darted left, down between the back of two houses. He heard car doors slam, and picked up speed. Other footsteps joined his own.

He turned again and then took a right; running past black-metal fire escapes that zigzagged up the high brick walls, weaving round bins and piles of rubbish. He didn't know it was a blind alley until he was at the end of it.

The bulb of a red exit sign at the top of one of the escapes lit the bricks a low fiery colour, lengthening the shadows. A cat screeched, knocking over a bin lid, and scarpered. Julius turned to watch it dart past and came eye to eye with the two goons who were standing between him and the only way out. One was very tall with a shiny, chiselled face and full lips, the other was short and wide with baggy cheeks and hang-dog eyes. They walked slowly towards him.

Julius tried to scream the word 'Help!' but his breath was balled up tightly in his throat and all he could get past it was a whisper. A chill feeling spread through the air.

The tall goon had a heavy jaw and the top of his head was slightly cone-shaped. He laughed and made a show of looking all around. 'Are you talking to us?'

The exit sign buzzed and flickered like an electric flytrap. The taste of fear was at the back of Julius's throat.

'Help,' he gasped again.

The tall goon did an impression of Julius's reedy cry and chuckled.

'All right, that's enough fooling around,' the wide goon snapped. 'Hand it over.'

'Please,' Julius whispered.

The goon's eyes darkened.

Julius quickly corrected himself. 'I meant, please don't take it. It's for the rent – if we don't pay up this week, we'll be out . . . we don't have anywhere else.'

The goon rolled his eyes and faked a yawn. He held out a hand and beckoned a 'gimme' with his fingers. 'Don't make me ask again,' he snarled.

To emphasise the point his companion pulled out a lead pipe and thumped it menacingly against the palm of his hand.

With trembling fingers Julius unzipped the money belt and threw it across the ground towards them. It rolled to just short of the wide goon's feet.

A shiver ran over Julius's skin, as a draught of cold air blew past.

The wide goon nodded impatiently at the belt and the tall goon stepped forward, and then stopped as a look of pure dread dawned on him. The exit sign blew.

A metal bin lid frisbeed out from behind Julius and hit the tall goon on the chest, beating him backwards. He fell onto the wide goon, knocking him into a mound of bin bags under the fire escape.

Julius turned to see who had come to his rescue, but there was no one there. He looked back again to see the goons shoving each other angrily as they scrambled to their feet, slipping on the contents of the burst bin bags.

'So he thinks he's a tough guy.' The tall goon raised his pipe threateningly at Julius.

'No – I . . .' Julius looked around for an

explanation but he couldn't find one so he fell silent.

'You're going to be sorry.' The tall goon rushed at him but something struck his shoulder and he spun round like a turnstile. His legs flipped out from under him and he went down, his pipe landing end up on his forehead. 'Yow!' he yelped, clutching his skull.

The wide goon bared his teeth as he strode towards Julius – and straight into the bin lid, which was in the air again. It struck him on the head like one half of a pair of cymbals. The goon reeled off against the slimy alley wall and pinned himself there.

'It's some kind of trick!' he yelled.

The money belt still lay on the floor. The tall goon began to crawl towards it, then his face paled and he crawled back again and onto his feet, staring at Julius in abject horror.

Julius shrugged helplessly at him and shivered.

The goons glanced quickly at each other then scarpered, their thumping boots followed by the strain of an engine starting and the screech of tyres – and they were gone.

Even when the sound of the car had faded, Julius Oliver hesitated, his heart racing, and then, very carefully, he walked forward. The money belt swooped up, skimming a puddle unsteadily and landed in his hands.

He stood there for a moment staring at the belt. Then he looked up and his eyes travelled around the empty alley.

When he finally spoke his voice was husky and had a tremble in it. 'You're him, aren't you? The one in the paper. The –' Instinctively he took a step away as the hair on the back of his neck stood on end. His breath curled out in front of him and drifted around in the darkness, and then his heart began to slow, the sweat cooling on his skin and his breathing quieting until all he could hear was the rustling of the rain.

Julius gulped. 'Hey, kid!' he called out into the darkness. 'Thanks!'

The icy air and the creepy feeling in the alley

began to fade and after a moment the Peligan City night returned to just being cold and dark again, but maybe not as cold or as dark as it had once been.

Acknowledgements

Karl James Mountford, my creative partner in crime for Potkin and Stubbs, for passion and generosity that went above and beyond.

Emma Matthewson, Jenny Jacoby, Tina Mories, Nick Stearn, Jane Harris and all the team at Piccadilly Press for believing in this story and helping to make these books the best they could be. Thank you for being in my corner.

For their literary map reading skills, clearing

the path and lighting the way: Hilary Delamere and Jessica Hare at The Agency; the unstoppable Meg Burrows; Liz Ferretti, Morag Clarke, Jane Bailey and Ruth Dugdall.

My colleagues at Suffolk Libraries, who I'm very proud to work alongside, for making it possible for me to juggle my dream jobs, and to my friends and family: thanks for cheering me on and keeping me going.

Potkin and Stubbs was inspired by many great hard-boiled and noir novels and films, including the work of Dashiell Hammett, Dorothy B. Hughes, Raymond Chandler and Vera Caspary, Humphrey Bogart, Alan Moore and the music of Billie Holiday, Miles Davis and Duke Ellington.

Sophie Green

Sophie Green writes children's fiction and short stories. She has a degree in zoology and an interest in folklore and urban legend. She was born and still lives in East Anglia and works as a librarian for Suffolk libraries.

Karl James Mountford

Karl James Mountford was born in Germany and is now a full-time illustrator based in Wales.

He studied illustration at Swansea College of Art and was also the artist in residence there while studying for his MA in Visual Communication.

He now spends most of his day illustrating all types of awesome stories and genres.

Piccadilly
P R E S S

Thank you for choosing a Piccadilly Press book.

If you would like to know more about our
authors, our books or if you'd just like to know
what we're up to, you can find us online.

www.piccadillypress.co.uk

And you can also find us on:

We hope to see you soon!